I

AM

THE

SUN

Destined Lore I

Aryrejin El

Works of Aryrejin El

WIND
*All My Messy Thoughts
and Open Doors*

Gentle Wild Things
*Here is My Heart,
Root Tangled and Wild*

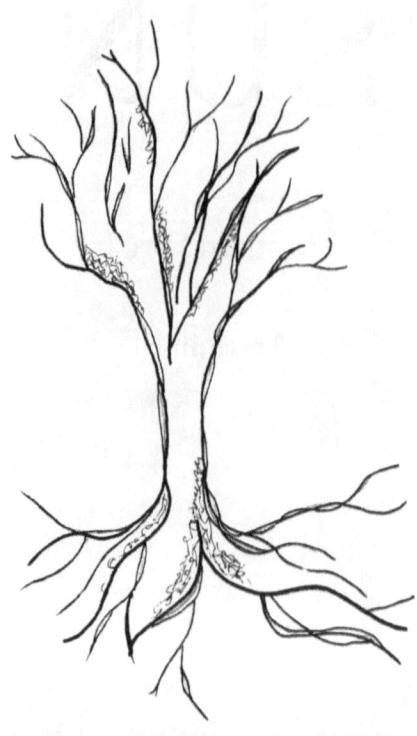

Dedication

For Hannah Grace

With my love

Note on the Characters

Etz:

Descended from tree. They appear human,
except for the boughs that horn their heads.
They have chlorophyll for blood.
They inhale carbon dioxide and exhale oxygen.
Some can grow leaves or vines from themselves,
yet most have lost this ability, along with being able to
command elements of nature.
As an Etz ages, they will become more tree-like, even
loosing their features and voices, until their body puts
down roots and they return to tree form. Centuries can
pass before another Etz is born from that tree, who will
bear a different name.
The consumption of pure light, Afyia, is vital for life.

Alom:

Descended from stone.They appear human,
yet most are the color of the stone they were born from.

They do not die, yet live as dust until they are able to
compact and take form again. Most remember their name
and will resume their previous identity when given new life.

Yahalom, or diamonds, are Alom born with the potential to
become diamonds under tremendous pressure. If conditions
are not right, Alom will shatter instead of shedding their
previous color and taking on the rainbow-hued Yahalom body.
The consumption of Afyia is vital for life.

Afyia and the Ion Trees:

Ion Trees gather light and vital energy from earth and sky,
transforming it into star-like fruits that glow when ripe.
Afyia is made from ions and other light sources depending on
the type being made. It can be any color, liquid or solid, and glows softly.
It is energizing and enriching for those who consume it, vital as water.
(Drinking in tea is highly recommended.)

Preface

Once, the Divine walked amongst us.

The stones were in awe of their Radiant Creator,

and lept from where they rested, running after the

light with their legs of jade and granite and diamond.

The Divine slept under trees and laid in deep,

grassy places. The trees had no wish to lose

the glorious song pouring from the Divine's lips,

so they pulled up their roots and bent down

their boughs to follow.

The Divine saw the determination and resiliance of

the two and knew that they were *tov,* good.

The Divine granted the trees a new name, *Etz.*

Giving them blood of chlorophyll and lungs of green,

they were allowed to walk and sing as

they so desired, eating the fruit of the ion trees.

Death would not find them, only bring them

back into their original form to live and

breathe as a tree once more.

For the stones, the Divine gave the name *Alom*,

after their strength and joy.

They would break and return to their

dust only to form again, for death was not for them.

They drank from the light of purity, Afiya,

and grew strong.

The *Etz* and *Alom* lived harmoniously, sharing

joy in their Creator.

Yet a darkness sprouted in the land, a poison the

angels could not fight. The Divine left to

preserve life in other realms.

"My Soul shall be among you,

continue to live well. Tov."

They forgot the Divine's words and the

little light of the ion trees grew scarce.

They dug Afiya from the ground and gathered

it from the skies. They tried to mimic the light of

the Divine One by building a distorted illumination.

Try as they might, they soon forgot the

love of the Divine in the face of turmoil.

They forgot the Soul of the Divine,

who watched them still.

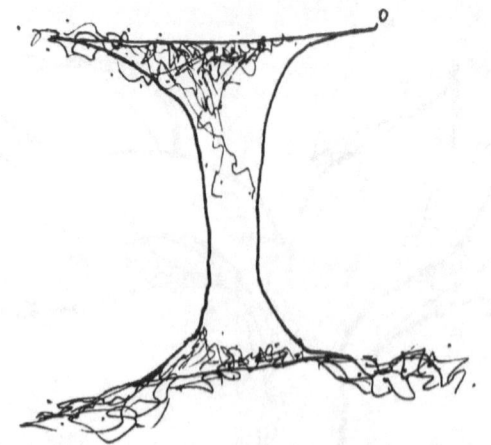

 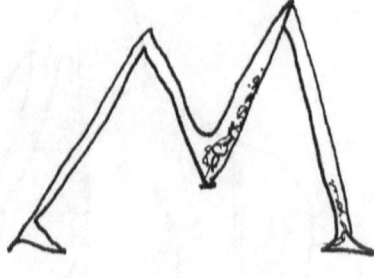

BELIEF

&

INK

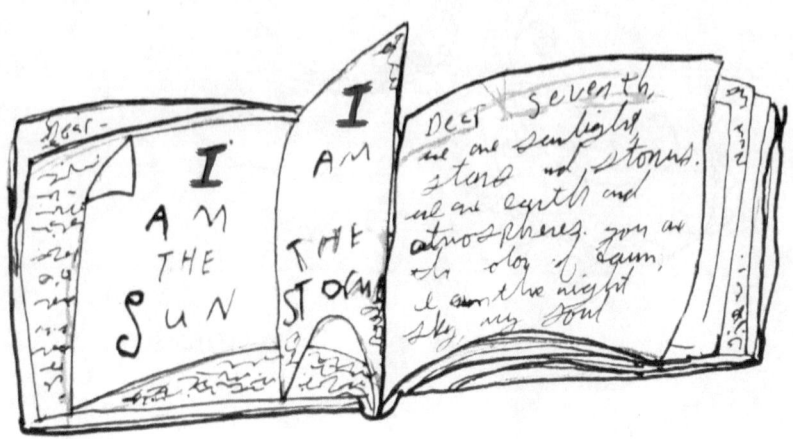

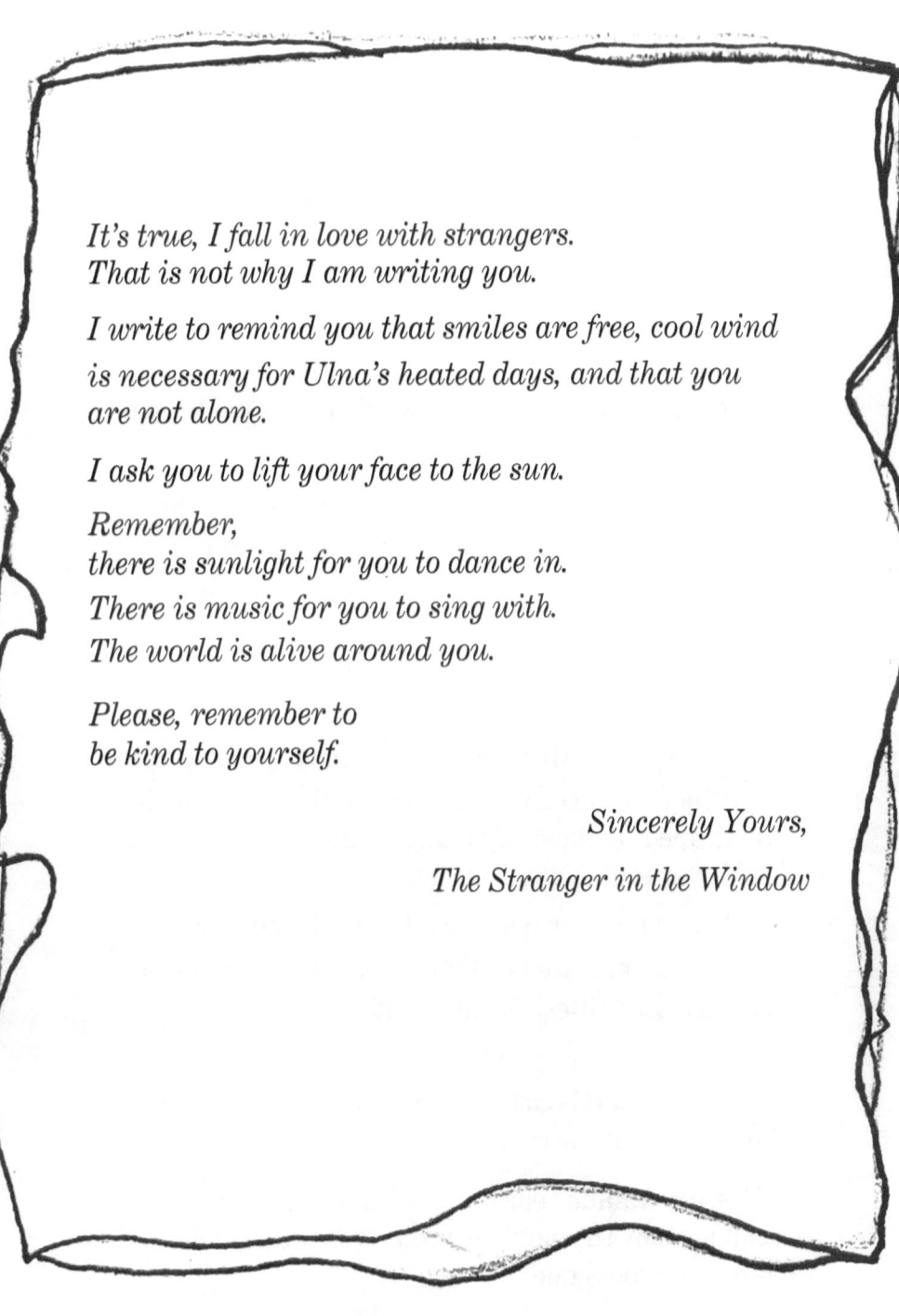

It's true, I fall in love with strangers.
That is not why I am writing you.

I write to remind you that smiles are free, cool wind
is necessary for Ulna's heated days, and that you
are not alone.

I ask you to lift your face to the sun.

Remember,
there is sunlight for you to dance in.
There is music for you to sing with.
The world is alive around you.

Please, remember to
be kind to yourself.

Sincerely Yours,

The Stranger in the Window

i.

There is no stranger in the window, no sun above her head, no music so she might dance.

Yet she closes her eyes, trying to remember the last song she heard. Yearning to comprehend how it must feel, to be warmed by the sun, standing in full light without fear.

Fear holds her breath captive; fights in her lungs for control.

"I'm trying." Alyce signs, her hands speaking the words her vocal cords cannot say to the silent gardens, still draped by the dewy blue of night.
The letter crumples in her fist.

A betraying tear falls from her dark cheek. For the first time, since her flight through dark streets and war-torn cities, she allows it.

"I'm trying to remember…what it means to smile." Her hands cast shadows over her body with their words. Their cry.

Her crystalline tear lands with a quiet *spat*, swallowed by the earth. Alyce leaves the gardens before the roots take form.

"How are you feeling today, Miss Chime?" A familiar voice breaks her thoughts.

Alyce startles, busy rubbing ink smudges between her fingers. Her nurse, an Etz, is tall with twisting boughs sprouting from a loose bun of verdant hair. Heritage of a willow, perhaps. Though she studied the tree-like people of Ulna extensively, it was hard to tell the difference in person. This woman could be descended from a weeping maple, or a wisteria vine.

Alyce puts her thumb between her first two fingers, tilting her wrist on its axis. Their sign for "Okay".

The nurse marks something down, meeting her eyes with soft purple ones. "Let's have a look at those wounds."

It's routine now. Pulling off her shift, redressing the burns extending from her shoulders with gauzy strips of cotton, then attending to the broken ribs on her right torso. Each breath is sharp, painfilled and tedious.

Alyce fumbles for paper and ink as they finish, lifting the page with shaky hands.

"Who writes the letters?" Her nurse reads her hurried scrawl, brushing a tendril of slender leaves from her brow. "I'm not entirely sure, it seems like

everyone around here gets one. No-" she laughs, reading Alyce's quick words. "They are not the same, from my understanding. I've never received one though."

She checks Alyce's weight, temperature, blood pressure, before leaving her alone in the dim lights of her room.

The new electric lights, compliments of the Sun King, put her on edge. Their frequency is rigid, disformed and near angry. She flinches, reaching for the switch, the movement of her thumb leaving her in semi darkness.

Little relief, the darkness gives. She sighs, the letter's sharp edges poking into her skin when she rolls slightly. Another agony, not being able to sleep on her side.

I ask you to lift your face to the sun... The words are a song. A hymn. When was the last time she sang? Spoke?

Alyce can remember speaking. Sounds striking off her tongue. But she cannot remember the last word she said...before the war started, or after it ended.

Alyce does not hide her curiosity when the second letter arrives, tucked under her breakfast bowl twelve days later. Already the first bares signs of wear, folded and refolded and the ink traced uncountable times.

She tugs it free, letting it sit in her hands like a promise, a love song to her own heart. The mystery of it only makes her faith in words grow. What will it tell her this time?

"Are you enjoying the letters?"

Alyce straightens, looking up through sooty lashes at her golden nurse. Boughs curl around his ears like ram horns, poking through golden curls, thick with bark. There are small green scars on his steady hands, which refill her blue water glass. Funny, he seems almost bashful, his dark eyes refusing to meet hers.

Alyce nods, and he brightens. That small smile is sunlight in her dim room.

"I recommend sitting outside today, the weather is clear and wonderful." His hands shake a little; he lifts away the pitcher.

Alyce nods again, unsure what to say and frustrated by her lack of voice.

He stands, hesitant and awkward for the usual self-righteous med staff of Halo Hospital. He nods once, departing with a small wave.

Alyce sighs, leaning back in bed. You'd think they'd give inexperienced nurses the easy patients. Regardless... his frequency was gentle and calm. She could have said something, written a thank you at least. Asked him to stay... Alyce turns away from the thought. He is Etz, she is Alom. She has woken up in an enemy hospital- their people are at war!

No. The war is over now. This need to draw lines must stop. Despite her fears, she must choose to take the first step.

She opens the letter.

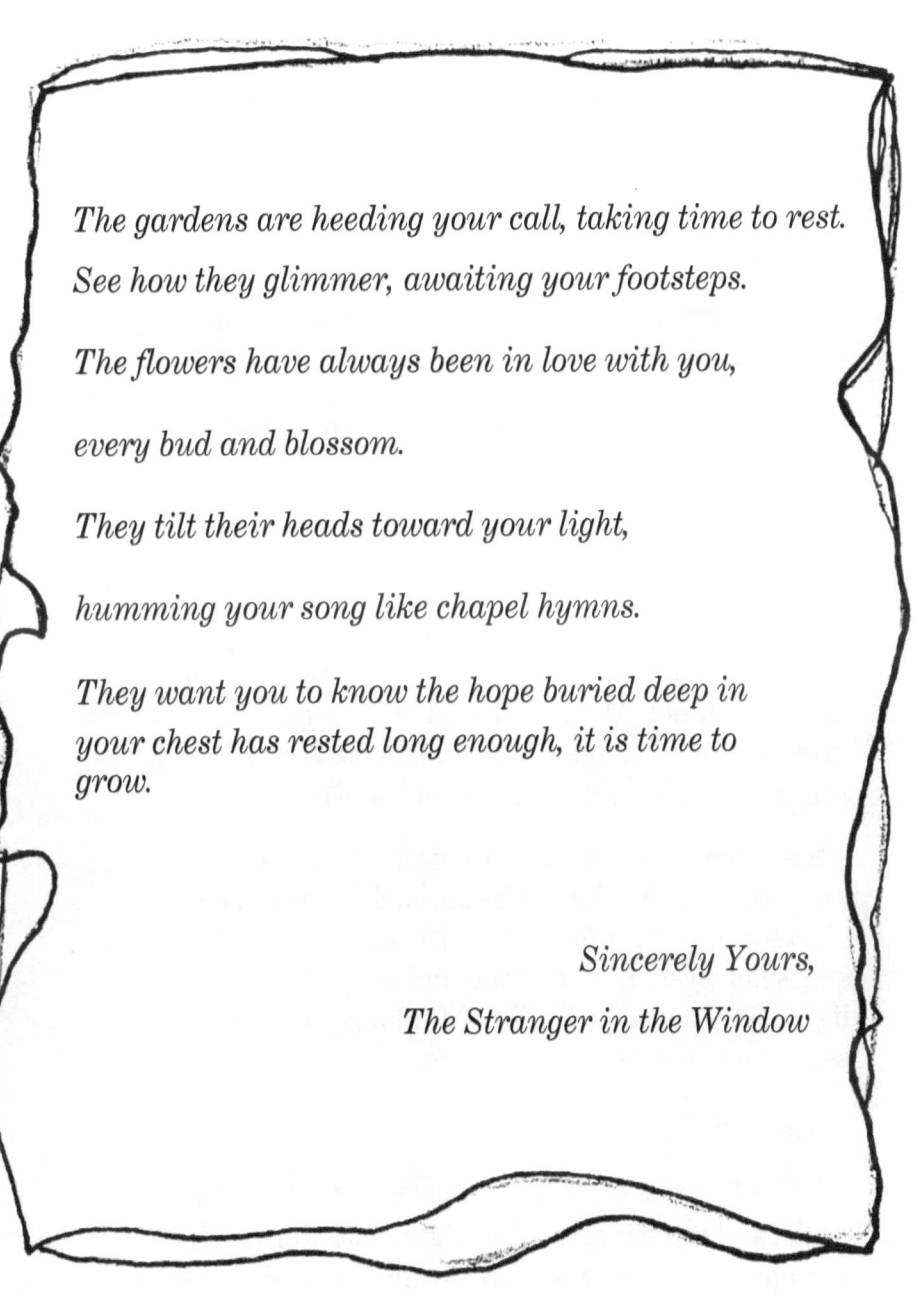

The gardens are heeding your call, taking time to rest.
See how they glimmer, awaiting your footsteps.

The flowers have always been in love with you,

every bud and blossom.

They tilt their heads toward your light,

humming your song like chapel hymns.

They want you to know the hope buried deep in
your chest has rested long enough, it is time to
grow.

Sincerely Yours,
The Stranger in the Window

Wind chimes spark and sing in the garden below. A child laughs on the lap of her father. An elderly man cries on the corner of his bench. There is a bird in the tree, nestling her littles.

Alyce feels tears well and drop, tracing lines down her cheeks.

This is the second time, she sobs, that she has cried over words.

She sniffs, pulling her emotions back in. She must remain silent. She must protect herself.

Especially here, amid the watchful eyes of Ulna's green blooded Etz.

She's grateful for the moss on her shoulders, the tiny yellow flowers blooming along her spine. The minerals of her Alom body capable of small growths. She's tangled roots in her hair, prays they resemble the hornlike boughs of the Etz.

She's too weak for them to discover she is Alom and exile her. No doubt the authorities have been alerted; they hunt for a girl with silver eyes. Alyce shuts her eyes, they are dull and grey without the light she craves. Jaal will not find her. He didn't search for her before, surely now is no different.

She stills her panic.

"This letter is beautiful." She signs to the air, the walls, and the windows shut tight. The words on her hands feel like breath, easy and needed.

"How long have I needed light? How long have I deprived myself out of fear and unrest? How much longer am I willing to exist in this darkness, pretend it is light?"

She's ringed the bell for the nurse before she can think. The lavendered eyed willow woman enters, peeking her head through the door, one hand wrapping the frame.

"Everything alright?" Willow signs, concern etching her features.

Alyce nods, covering her disappointment. The boy of gold is gone. Alyce pulls in a shaky breath, her lungs working against the sharp tug of pain.

"May I have some paper? And a pen?"

Willow smiles at her request.

ii.

Fire. Burning against his legs, his back, his hands. He is consumed.

Smoke burns his eyes and pain throbs in his head. Emerald blood, so deep it is liquid ink, pours from his arteries. Chlorophyll splattered onto the earth.

"Ojo." His voice hoarse, he can barely hear himself.

"Ojo!" A shrill cry echoes across the battlefield, awaking Percy from his nightmarish sleep.

A hand crosses his brow, rests on his head. Lips quivering, he takes in the slate grey paint, the cream curtains, the wide frame containing splattered art, his brother's signature along the bottom. His trusty spider plant reaches a tendril toward him in concern.

"I'm okay, thanks buddy." Percy taps his thumbs against a long leaf.

The leaf taps him back.

Exhaling, Percy falls back into his pillows, lingering uncomfortably in the sweat soaking his sheets.

"I should shower, huh?" Percy smiles at his friend, who gives an affirming shimmy.

Percy laughs, lighting up his dark room. Arms wide, he tosses the window open, leaning onto the ledge. Wind tugs on golden curls, wraps around his quivering fingers.

"It's alright now. You're safe."

"I know." He speaks to the wind. "It's just hard to believe."

Water streams down his back, over his closed eyelids and pruned hands. Suds form over his chest and body, he rubs soap into his hair, cleans each grove and twist of his boughs. The water starts to grow cold and he leans his head out the sheer curtain and hollers down the hall.

"Sol! My water!"

"Ah, you'll spoil yourself with all that heat." A voice grumbles back.

"Or maybe I'd just like a hot shower for once!"

"Boy, it's been thirty seven minutes-"

Percy rolls his eyes while a grin spreads over his face. But Sol is right, he'll be late. Drying off, he dresses in loose pants, a pale shirt, sleeves rolled to his elbows.

The stairs creak as he pounds down them, Sol covers his ears from the kitchen sink.

"My poor stairs." The older man mutters, shaking his head. "You want breakfast?"

"No." Percy tugs on his coat. "I'm late as it is."

"At least take an Afiya to go- Waiden!"

"Catch you later, old man!" Percy flies out the door, leaving it agape. He might catch the train if he ran or, nope. There's the horn.

"Ugh!" He rubs a hand into his forehead, slowing his pace. Wind circles his head, easing the throb. The air is gentle, cool and clean. Perhaps a walk might not be so bad...

"Percy Waiden! You are late-"

"I know, I'm sorry. I had to catch the late train." Percy throws off his coat, grabbing a white hospital gown, fastening it around his waist. "I'll work late tonight-"

"And be dragging your feet in exhaustion, I don't think so." His boss gives him a firm stare. "I try to keep my beds empty rather than full." Rossi blows a tight curl from her emerald bark cheek. "Just help Frost, we're short staffed."

"On it." Percy is down the hall before she has another critique on his time management.

Percy waves to the few patients who have their doors open, some smile and others scowl, looking away. A small spike of anxiety travels down his spine. Percy reminds himself everyone has their story, words stored in their hearts, scars carved into life lines. His fingers itch to hold a pen.

"Daydreaming again, Waiden?" Frost pokes his head into Percy's vision quick as lightning. He startles, straightening his coat.

"Just thinking." That easy smile he uses crosses his face, effortless and practiced. Fake. He wipes sweaty palms on his pants. "What do you need?"

Frost sighs, dropping his stiff stance. "Room four has been up since two and cranky." Green eyes crinkle in irritation.

"Mabel? She's so nice-"

"Room seven has yet to wake from surgery and the doc is stopping by later today, one of us will need to be in attendance. Room eight-" Frost laughs sarcastically, running a hand through silver flecked locks, "left her room only once. Refuses our

14

Afiya. Refuses sunlight, electric lights, even candles!" Frost throws up his hands as if preaching, condemning the masses to sin.

"Some Etz are afraid of fire, Frost-" Percy tries to sooth, pulling carbon dioxide in even lungfulls, counting down from a hundred as Frost continues.

"This isn't fear, Waiden, she doesn't want light ions at all. She'll be in bigger trouble if she doesn't have some Afiya-"

"What would you like me to do?" He keeps his voice crisp. Professional.

"Take four and seven. Jasmine has been popping in and out of eight but do me a favor and at least get some form of light in there or Rossi will have my bark. I'll take the other patients."

Percy shivers before entering room four, plastering a cheerful smile on his face, hoping the lingering nightmare doesn't show.

He opens the door hesitantly, unsure of what to expect and-

The woman lay sobbing on the floor.

Percy skids to her side, landing on his knees with a thud. "Are you alright? Why are you on the floor, ma'am?"

Hands grip his shirt, fumbling and quivering. "I- I cannot see! Where am I?"

"It's alright-" He places careful hands on her shoulders, steadying her.

"How is this alright?!"

"Ma'am, please calm down, it *is* going to be alright. I promise. You're in the hospital."

She stills at his words.

"You've had a concussion and temporarily lost your sight."

"Why can't I remember anything?" Her fists tighten.

"The doctors think it is the trauma. Your memories come and go, along with your sight. You've been getting hypnosis treatment and had surgery to release pressure on the brain. You are going to be alright, Mabel. May I call you Mabel?"

She nods, Percy starts to stand, pulling her up after him. "Now, let's get you back in bed."

Percy rests her on the edge of the bed. Mabel fumbles a dark hand in the sheets before scooting back and laying down. Fetching a glass of water, Percy hovers over her as she gulps it down gratefully.

"I… remember being admitted now, it must have been my panic." She laughs awkwardly. "I'm sorry."

"Not at all. I heard you haven't been sleeping well."

She nods, her blue eyes vacant. "Nothing happy to dream about, I'm afraid." She grips a small stuffed flower in her hands. "Is this a child's toy?" Fingers dig in the felt and loose stitching. Suddenly her eyes widen before Percy can speak.

"I have a son. I remember holding him! What is his name?"

"Chalo." Percy smiles. "He visited yesterday and is expected tomorrow."

"Chalo." She breathes. "Yes. How could I have forgotten his name?" Her sobs start anew, quiet and painful. Percy rubs his chest, aching on the inside.

Hesitating, his hand rests on hers. "He loves you. He says so every time he visits. Your husband does too."

"I remember Hallan…" her hand drifts to the union mark on her forehead. A small circle, signifying their marriage.

She tilts her head to Percy. "My family is safe?"

He nods, habit. "Yes," his words quick.

Percy straightens, taking the stethoscope from his pocket. "May I?"

Mabel nods. Percy presses the large, round scope to her heart, leaning his ear against the smaller, protruding side.

"A perfect beat." He proclaims.

"You are a better nurse than that other guy."

"Frost?" Percy laughs, surprised. "He's more experienced than I am."

"Hm, you are kinder. And cuter, I can tell." She winks milk pale eyes.

"I don't know about that, you should see the line of Etz at his door." Percy adds conspiratorially, then winces, realizing his mistake. Relief floods through him when she laughs, a smile blooming over her honey hued face.

After administering meds, marking Mabel's chart, and tiding up the room, Percy places a hand on her arm, speaking softly.

"I'll check up on you again, have a good morning, Mrs. Mabel."

"You too, dear."

"Thanks." Percy wipes his cheeks, surprised to find stray tears soaking into his fingers. He closes her door with a soft click.

He stands for a moment in the hallway, memories overcoming his functioning, ion bright and pulling him down. Down. Down.

Percy shakes his head. Ojo's smile and chattering words lost to him once more.

He rounds the hall, stumbling over his feet. Doctor Hill scowls in room seven's doorway, clicking a pen over his board.

Percy smooths his coat, resists the temptation to bury his hands in oversized pockets.

"I'm not pleased with this recovery. He should have woken." Hill taps his note board, conducting a song of panic and urgency.

"Perhaps if we slowed the meds," Percy suggests quietly. "The pain sedatives could be overloading the body, forcing him into further comatose-"

"Meds are billable, but a sleeping patient, wasting our bed, is not." The doctor practically growls.

Percy clenches his fists, holding the retort in his mouth like iron. Until it becomes too heavy and spews out anyway. "A patient whose vitals are this good does not need seven different medications, they can go to someone else."

"And a volunteer nurse has no right to speak to me about such matters. You haven't even finished med school-"

"Been a little busy saving lives on the *army medical team* and fighting for my country. Why are *you* here?"

Hill's eyes bulge at his interruption.

The doctor glares, shooing Percy away, flicking lint from his coat like he didn't just lose to an undergraduate kid. "You are dismissed from my presence."

His fists tighten, but he doesn't speak. The doctor disappears down the hall with a click of polished shoes.

Percy breathes through his nose, out through his mouth. Even. Controlled. Ten deep breathes will change the carbon dioxide in the brain and he will feel peace.

Ten. Twenty. Fifty.

Percy works his way to the rest room before his anxiety takes form.

"I am so fired." Percy buries his face in his hands. Tells himself he is trembling with exhaustion, or maybe low blood sugar. Darn it, he should have eaten…

"Am I fired?"

"Of course not." Frost says from the sunlamp stall, lounging on an electronic light bed. "You're a volunteer, they can't fire you."

"They could ask me not to come back. Refuse my application. Lock me from the building."

"That is a little dramatic." Frost stands, Percy kicking the door closed while Frost changes, the stall opens a second later revealing a perfect swish of silver hair and pristine clothing.

"Doc Hill is a jerk, true, but he means well. Sometimes."

"Well, not anymore." Percy splashes water on his face, wiping his chin with a rough towel.

"You stood up for someone, that matters more than your position." Frost grips his shoulders, giving an encouraging shake.

"You're right." Percy nods, fastening the top of his coat, eyeing Frost's grip. "Did you wash your hands?"

"Anyway-" Frost turns on the faucet, suds forming over opaque, aspen hands. "I'll always have your back."

"Huh, usually you discourage me from doing things."

"That's not the point."

"It doesn't matter who it is, we are not a hospital based on money and greed, Halo has always been about helping people- even if we don't see a dime from the work."

"Times are changing." Frost shrugs. "The King demands more from hospitals and corporations. Ion prices rising due to the Stonefloor. People are scared."

"I know! I know." Percy rubs his temples, the stress of it all making his heart race. One of the reasons he volunteered was to stay *busy*. Anything was better than sitting at home and wondering which way the world was going to tilt. Which side he would end up on and how he would repair all the wounds he had caused.

"I'll talk to Rossi, explain what happened. The patient comes first, above all else."

Frost studies him for a moment. "Let me. I'm your supervisor, I'll send in a formal complaint. Hill needs to learn that inside these walls, money should not matter."

"Frost, what is that?" Percy points to his perfectly formed cheek, a red patch blooming into a burn before his eyes.

Frost winces, touching the new wound. "Odd, I would have noticed getting this."

"Do you think...?" Percy eyes the sunlamp stall, built by the King's orders to lessen Afiya consumption and ion use.

"Nah, the King claimed testing was done first. He wouldn't have given us these if they were harmful. I must have…bumped into something."

"Super plausible." Percy sighs, "I should go, I still need to check on room eight. Does anyone have her name yet?"

"No." Frost blows a lock of hair from his face. "The only one who can sign is Jasmine. Either the girl hasn't wanted to say or Jasmine isn't filling out all her reports. Man-" Frost sighs, running fingers through his hair. "I'm too busy to think."

"Curious." Percy muses.

"She was found stranded in the battlefield, unconscious and wounded. She's a fighter." Frost chuckles. "You'd think someone would come looking for her. I couldn't tell which side she was on when she was brought in. Such strange energy."

"The wounded are the wounded."

Frost laughs, placing a hand on his shoulder. "And I'm the King's lost son."

Percy says nothing, remembering the girl's sad, grey eyes. How they sparked when she received the letter under her breakfast bowl. That was four days ago now.

He should have learned sign language.

The soft pulse of energy emanating from room eight matches the beat of his heart, rhythmic and calm. He tries to coax his messy curls into something reasonable looking, (instead of the 'mad scientist' vibe usually haloing him. His white coat doesn't help.)

"Hello?" He knocks, turning the door quietly. The girl is asleep in her bed, lashes inky dark against her charcoal skin. Percy smiles. The hazy light spilling from the curtains causes her freckles to glow softly, as if she were a star. No, glimmering and silver as the whole night sky.

Percy shakes himself, focusing on his checklist. Check Vitals. Get out. Don't be weird.
Vitals good. Check.
Cleaning and rebandaging wounds and meds to be administered by Jasmine in two hours. Check. The room is... in need of a cleaning.
Percy studies her face again, the thin, intertwining boughs wrapping her head like a crown. Interesting...

Percy closes his eyes, listening, feeling for the energy of life surrounding all things.

These boughs, they are not breathing, not beating with life, as if they are dead roots dug up from barren ground.

Being weird, check- No! He internally chides himself.

Percy shuffles, parchment caught under foot. There are papers and ink scrawling's and newssheets covering the bed, clutched in her hand and scattered on the floor. Percy lifts a few from the floor.

A newspaper heading reads Sun Prince Still Missing- His majesty King Usis has placed rewards for anyone who has information regarding the Prince's possible location. Along with the blurry picture of a boy in a painted mask.

Percy snorts. None had ever seen the boy's face outside of palace walls, and during every public event the young Prince always wore a mask, concealing parts of his face.

Percy shifts the page, hand written letters staring up at him.
Dear Stranger

The paper is snatched from his hand. Percy meets glaring, grey eyes. She signs something, angry and quick.

Percy puts his hands up. "Sorry, I didn't mean to intrude. Would you mind writing what you said?

Here." He pulls a small note pad from his pocket, flipping past horrible poetry to an empty page.

She scribbles furiously. *"Do you always intrude on the thoughts of others?"*

Percy gives an ironic grin at the words. Caught red handed. Check.

(The list is getting longer than he intended.)

"I apologize, just thought I'd tidy up a little. I was curious though, I'll admit."

She gives him a long stare, then sighs, her thin shoulders dropping.

"It's alright." She holds up the note pad for him to read. Her eyes find his, drift to his curling boughs, drop to her lap. She gathers the pages into her hands, cheeks pink.

"Here, I'll help. I promise I won't read any." Percy bends down, snatching the papers and turning them backwards before handing them to her.

"You like to write?"

"It's a new hobby."

Percy smiles. "I've been writing before I could read. My mom pen dictations for me. Little stories and songs. It's fun. Sometimes." He shrugs, wincing at the awkwardness of his unending words.

"Necessary too, like carbon dioxide or sunlight. I don't think I could live without words. They do drive me a little crazy on occasion." He laughs, though it dies in his throat when she barely bats an eye.

"How are you feeling?" He changes the subject.

"*Okay.*"

"Well, that's...good. Mind giving me a little more information than that?"

Her gaze is sharp and cutting, his cheeks flush suddenly.

He scratches one curved bough. "Are you in any pain? Do you need anything? I heard you've barely been outside, or used the sunlamps.

Healing will take longer without light-"

"*I don't like the electricity.*" She holds up the pad.

"Yeah, it's different. But the King assured us this is better than drinking Afiya. Uses less ions," he adds. Why is he defending the King's invention when he saw the burn on Frost's cheek?

"*You use sunlamps?*" She raises a brow, fingers quivering on the pad.

Percy shakes his head. "The only exposure I have is working here. I live in the country."

"*That sounds nice.*"

"It is." He sits in the lone chair. She's turned the page, pen awaiting her next thoughts. "Where do you live?"

She looks down, pen quiet, hovering, before writing quickly. She doesn't look at him as he reads.

"My home was destroyed."

"I'm sorry."

She nods, swallowing, fingers rigid and white knuckled. *"I lived in the city before. I enjoyed feeling the heart of activity and adventure alongside so many strangers. But not anymore."*

"Which city?"

"It doesn't matter now. It's gone too."

Percy wipes his hands on his pants, praying she cannot see how he shakes. "I'm Percy."

She hesitates. Eyeing him up and down, pen flicking over her fingers in a looping spiral.

"You don't have to tell me your name if you don't want to."

"Chime. Mother said I sounded like a bell to her. Humming. My given name is Alyce."

"Alyce Chime." Percy speaks aloud, the smile growing on his face, reaching his heart. "It's beautiful."

Alyce blushes. *" I'm sure you have other patients who need you. I wouldn't want to keep you."*

"I do, have other patients. But you can keep me anytime you want to."

Her blush deepens, crimson on her onyx cheeks.

"I mean, I'm open anytime you want to talk, or hang out, or need any writing advice." He's stammering, standing with sweating palms. "I'm just going to…open this for you."

Alyce flinches as he opens the curtains, streams of light falling onto her bed.

"Please get some light, Miss Chime. Jasmine will be in shortly."

Alyce nods, her eyes closed, hands clutching his poetry book. Percy smiles to himself. She really is like a star, bathed in all that light.

"I'm home!" Percy calls wearily, taking off his shoes at the door.

Sol rounds the corner, shoving a jar of water into Percy's hands. "I bet you haven't had enough to drink today and probably did lousy at your job due to low blood sugar." Sol tisks, hands on his labradorite hips. Percy takes a swig from the jar, gagging at the taste. "What is in this?" He coughs.

"Some electrolytes," Sol calls over his shoulder, already heading back into the kitchen.

"Why does it taste-"

"And some salt. It's good for you."

"Yeah, but-"

"A little bentonite clay, for detoxing. And lavender. For my stress."

Percy rolls his eyes, taking only a small sip before returning the cap. That should be drunk sparingly.

"What's for dinner?" Percy rounds the foyer, ducking to enter the kitchen.

"Not you, I hope." Sol snorts, tossing ground earth in a bowl. "You reek of electricity."

"It's not that bad-"

"All those odd frequencies. It's enough Earth is struggling to keep up with the advancing Stonefloor, now She'll have this to deal with too." Sol mutters under his breath, his grey stone skin holding halos of auroras. Soft blues and sparking greens, the rare flash of purple.

Percy removes his bag, careful not to make a sound. He did not want another lecture today.

"At least you showed up on time today, while dinner is hot, I mean."

"Is it actually hot this time?" Percy gasps, Sol rolls his eyes at the sarcasm.

Bowls are set, Percy rolls his spoon through the liquid light, thick with sprinkled minerals.

"Sol," Percy starts hesitantly, afraid to voice his troubling thoughts. "Would an Alom ever…disguise themselves?"

"What makes you ask?" Sol stuffs his face with a paler light than Percy's, taken from moon flowers and morning dew.

Percy takes a slow bite, light rich on his tongue. Oranges and cherries.

"I suppose, if they feel threatened. Alom tend to hide themselves during times of stress and fear. Why do you think most of the war was fought underground?"

Not all of the war, though. Percy doesn't speak, blinking the flashing images of burning cities from his mind.

"The end of a war is a complicated matter." Sol shakes his head, takes another bite.

"Lines that were once impenetrable now must be crossed for the benefit of peace. Everyone is scared and uncertain how to take the first step. Earth knows the King isn't doing anything to help."

Percy doesn't respond to Sol's jeering of the Sun King, though every part of him agrees.

Afiya soup blooms on his tongue, rich with ions and natural elements, illuminating his body from within.

"But if one was on neutral ground, safe from both sides, why continue to hide?" Percy gestures with his spoon, Sol slurps down the rest of his bowl.

"You're not in a position to assume what someone else has been through."

"Nor would I." Percy responds.

"I'm just saying," Sol holds up his hands for peace. "If healing is the path you have taken, then let that be your focus. Not the pain that caused the wounds, but the joy that comes through healing. You cannot grow a new garden full of dead weeds."

Percy finishes, hardly feeling the energizing ion light coursing within him, distracted by the cloud of ink in his mind.

"I'll wash." He stands, clearing the table.

Sol shakes his head, weaving him off. "I'm making some Afiya for tomorrow. Leave it."

The stairs creak under Percy's weight. There's a dent in the wall from one of his boughs, the faded blue paint chipped. Percy touches the crater, memories flooding his brain.

He'd been sick with a fever and bedridden shortly after his arrival, much to Sol's chagrin.

By his fourth day, the illness had only grown and Sol pulled him from bed, bouncing his sick form down the stairs and, somehow, (with supernatural labradorite strength, according to Sol,) deep into the woods.

He woke bleary-eyed and frightened, under the care of the treelike healer, Sara, hidden in the woods.

Percy smiles, shaking his head. Maybe that was the first moment, amid her bottles of Afiya and piercing glances, that he chose something for himself. The herbs of the earth healing him more than medicine or King Usis' electricity ever could.

He returned to Sol's rundown inn wanting something for himself, wanting to be a healer.

How far he has grown from that young soldier he used to be.

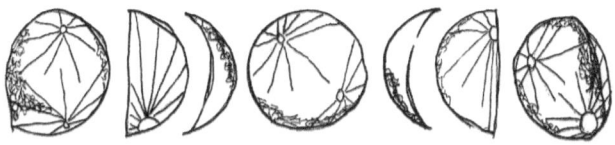

Alyce struggles against her dream. Hands balled in sweat-soaked sheets, she fights to wake.

Panic has replaced the light in her veins. Fear courses through her mind, her bones and arteries. She's drowning from the inside out.

Inky fingers pull her under, force her to bathe in the worst moments of her life. Memories trace patterns across her mind.

Her city is on fire, her home. Her King doesn't extinguish the flames, but gathers her people, forcing them under the sea.

"I love the sun too much." She remembers saying. *"Do not make me exist in such darkness."*

"It is the only way I can protect you-" Jaal spoke. Screamed. Shattered her with words. She ran from that too. Words.

Blearily she smudges liquid from her eyes, waking with exhaustion weighting her bones.

Wind tiptoes softly into her room, kissing her cheeks with pale lips, whispering of twilit gardens and high stars.

Alyce slips from her bed, creaking her door open, the sun not yet awake. Quiet hall, electric sunlamps flicker above head. Her face a grimace, she tiptoes from the room. Relief, her shoulders relaxing as she enters the quiet gardens. The pulse of the earth overpowers the tilting frequency of false lights.

Alyce sighs, careful of her wounds as she lies back in the cool grass. Shadowed benches line a stone pathway. Pruned trees, aching to be abandonedly wild, tower above her, silent sentinels, guardians of rest.

Alyce breathes in the lingering scent of night. Of humming earth and soft skies.

Alyce rests in the heartbeat of Earth, curled up in a hospital garden. Her frequency is the electron in an Atom, the heart of a mountain, the center of the sun. Her body is the moon, the ocean, reflecting the star light.
I am pieces of shattered stars.

Alyce sits upright, pulling pen and wrinkled paper from her pocket with an urgent need.

Frantically, her words start to flow.

I am pieces of shattered stars,
hiding my light from you.
I'd take you in my arms, let you to search
within me until you find the sun, for I am
galaxies and universes.
Yet I do not wish to burn you.

You are the sun, you will whisper.

I am the sun, I'll reply,
yet my body is the moon on a new night-
no light to be seen.

I am trapped within myself. I cannot be free.

The paper tears under her force, her pen shaking. She pokes a dark finger through the rip.

Perhaps she steals light, she thinks. She is not the sun. She is a black hole.

You must stay away from me, dear sun, lest I steal
your light.

Devour you like the darkest sea.

You will drown within me.

Alyce taps the newest poem into her growing pile, stuffed into the small book Percy gave her.

"Will you forever be silent?" Her breath sinches, the warm voice familiar, ethereal. Shame courses through her. They haven't spoken in so long.

"I want to speak again." She responds in her soul. The garden silent around her. The voice of the Divine a humming bell, chiming gently and soft as water.

"You are not using your words for kindness or purpose."

36

"Must I use them for anything other than self-expression?" She almost snaps, exhaustion weighing her down.

"Yes."

As if a chain has snapped from her neck, releasing her from a prison of silence, Alyce takes in a gulping breath. Another. Air pure and rich. She has been drowning, lost in a dark ocean, now she surfaces through the storm, lifted toward nebulas and radiant halos.

The Divine presses into her. She breathes impossibly deeper. This is her first breath. Her first moment of a new life, filled with the Divine's exhale.

Fingers of light rippling, burning through the darkness in her soul. Setting her free.

"I've missed you." Her first words, spoken aloud. How long has it been now? A sob bubbles in her throat. "I am sorry."

"There is nothing to apologize for. There is a reason you are here."

Hope rises in her, a new bud, shooting upward, toward divine light. "I am listening."

Beauty in pure form greets her, whispering over her mind, into her soul. Instructing guidance. She bathes in holy light, pieces of her soul restored in a song of light. She basks in divine essence as long as she dares, relishing the feel of deep love consuming her whole.

She rises just as the sun climbs over earth's curve, returning to the darkness of Halo Hospital.

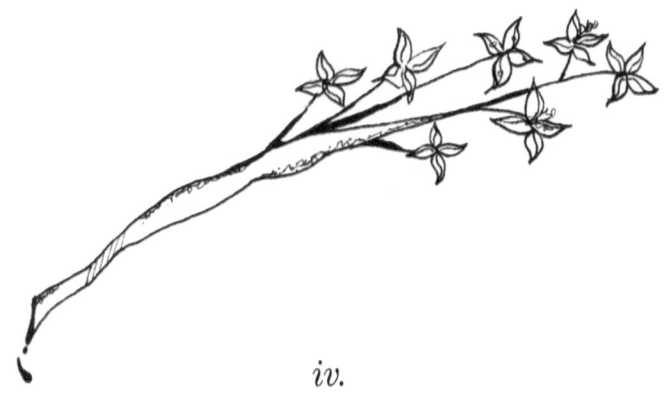

iv.

There's a letter in the trash. His feet are concrete; Percy cannot move.

To The Stranger in the Window curls before him in a familiar, flowing script.

Someone... wrote him back? He used to receiving little gratitude notes in the beginning, when he first started writing and leaving letters across the city, but that was years ago now. He hadn't heard from anyone in...well, a long time. Since before the war. But that writing... it couldn't be.

Percy pulls it from the trash, shaking filth from its corners.

"Aha!" Wind snatches it from his grasp, lifting it into the air. Circling higher and higher, a feather loose from the weight of bones. He's taken two giant steps forward, intending to chase it when-

"Waiden! What are you doing?"

Percy halts, staring back in an awkward pose at Rossi. His boss leans against the wall, spinning navy Afiya in a jar before taking a swig.

"I hope you're coming to work on time, not running down the street in…" her gaze narrows. "Are those pajamas?"

Percy flushes, fixing his pose. "No. Slacks."

Rossi rolls her eyes. "Just get inside."

"Yes, boss." Percy tucks his head as he passes. A finger to his shoulder stops him.

"You did right, with Hill. Sloppy about it, though." Rossi tilts her head back once more, twisting boughs rake the wall, light pouring into her throat as she drinks. "Next time, no scenes, just come to me."

Percy nods, slipping past her and inside. The wave of electricity hits him as the door closes, and he takes a moment to gather his bearings.

"You okay, Waiden?" Frost takes his shoulders, stabilizing him. Percy opens his eyes slowly.

"Not adjusting well to the sunlamps today. That's all."

He pulls away from Frost, afraid he will see the thoughts inside him. Memories crowding to the surface. He shakes himself. Get to work, Percy. He chides.

"What's needed for today?"

Frost shrugs. "It's quiet so far. The gal in room eight is actually *reading* to the boy in room seven. I

39

don't know if it's helping, but it's keeping them both occupied." Frost laughs at his own joke.

"Reading?" Percy frowns.

"Yeah." Frost chuckles. "Jasmine told me this morning. She's been speaking all day."

"I'll check in with them, then go my usual rounds."

Frost nods disinterested, already scanning over the schedule for the day.

Percy steadies his breath as he walks. *Speaking?* His brain is spinning and he doesn't know if it's from the electric lamps, the letter that *cannot possibly* be real, or the fact that the girl who has been mute for the past two weeks suddenly can speak.

He stops just outside the door, hand hovering, ready to knock.

"'I held my breath as I stood over the cliff.

I wanted to remember what it felt like to breathe again.

My lungs fill and hold; pressure within me.

I will be the force of the sea when I exhale, I will be the hurricane upon the shore.

I will be the birth of planets and the death of stars.

I am everything- all in a hushed breath I slowly release, rocking the world with my touch.'"

He knocks.

Pages and shuffling, the screech of a chair. Why is he frozen? Percy taps his fingers against his palm. Today is rolling away from him, at least his mind is.

Alyce answers the door, grey eyes timid. "Hello." Her voice is soft, but a smile grows on her lips.

"Hello." Percy wipes his hands, fingers trembling. By Earth, her voice is beautiful. A bell, a singing star.

"I'm here to…just check in." He winces at his words, how awkward. Flashes of memories he doesn't want to relive flicker and grow behind his eyelids.

"Are you alright?" Alyce touches his arm, bringing him back to his body, the hospital, her hand traveling to his knuckles, thumb idly tracing green scars. She snatches her hand away when his gaze lands on her fingers.

"Fine."
He stumbles, Alyce's hands slamming into his shoulders, stopping his fall.

"Obviously not." She grunts, guiding him onto her paper scattered chair.

"I'm s-sorryy." He slurs. Unfocused eyes slipping over the sleeping boy's chest, locking on the rising and falling of lungs. Percy tries to match the rhythm.

Alyce rushes to the small sink, getting him a cup of water.

She presses it into his hand, her own cupped over his. He's trembling.

His vision flickers in and out. Irongun shots and fire burn in his mind. A city falls. His brother's death. It's his fault. Why would he let his baby brother join the army? What kind of a brother is he? Terrible. A terrible one.

His left leg bounces uncontrollably.

"Should I call someone?"

"No." He gets out, a shout; his words must be heard over the noise in his head.

He puts his head into his hands. "No. It'll pass. Please, I need it to pass…" He doesn't speak the last words to her. Sending them out to Whoever may be listening. Praying this panic over taking him flees.

His mind plays wicked games, returning him to the worst moments of time. To the loss of identity and family. Chlorophyll blood dark upon his hands. Ojo…

Percy doesn't know how long he sits there, losing all sense of control and time. His mind is racing and all he wants is everything to stop.

He blinks, hours or minutes later, he's unsure. There's a cool rag on his neck and draping the pulse points in his wrists. The fog lifting, he raises his head. Alyce hovers over him, a hand on his shoulder.

"How do you feel?"

He groans, trying to gain control of words. His vision blurs and refocuses. "How long...?"

Alyce checks the clock. "Maybe thirty minutes, forty."

Percy nods, leaning back in the chair. "I'm sorry, that was so unprofessional." He laughs; her face remains serious.

"You fought in the war."

A shaky breath. "Yes."

She doesn't ask anything after that, just looks down at the boy. "We should let him rest, poor dear."

She bends, gathering sheets and sheets of poetry and music scores and Percy's small book where they stored their first words.

"Will you walk me to my room?" Alyce asks, smiling.

"You're joking, of course I will." Percy tries to smile but it's a grimace. Alyce helps him from the chair, strength firing in her small form. She slings an arm over her shoulder, hoisting him up.

"No, Miss Chime, your wounds."

"I'm bound up pretty good, trust me."

"I will after I check them myself."

She laughs.

Oh, her voice. It is the ocean at dawn. The sun breaking through grey skies. It ignites something in his chest. Breaking down his barrier of fear and functionality.

Alyce walks him from room seven, swinging open her own room, letting Percy support himself on the jam. She bustles, setting her papers aside, fetching him another blue glass of water.

He presses the rim to his lips. "I wish they'd use pure water. This is polluted from war."

"I know." Alyce scrunches her face at the mention of hospital water. Seven deep breaths, ten. His mind clears a little more, following her movements. Like a dancer she cleans up the floor and small work area, passing him glances as he leans against the frame, finishing the rest of his water.

"How do you feel now?" She's clutching a piece of paper in her dark fist, illuminated by the passing daylight. She seems to *glow* from within, a fire. Her skin is ash, coal and dust, hiding this light. Protecting her.

"What happened, Alyce. To your voice?"

She looks down. Touches her throat. A shaky, relieving sigh and her shoulders drop. A smile touches the corner of her lips, then she remembers his presence and shrugs, shy again.

"Have you always been able to speak? This whole time?"

She shakes her head. "No. This morning I…" she laughs and it's genuine, "the Divine Hum broke the chains over my voice." She says each word with reverence. A prayer.

Percy doesn't speak. She presses the folded paper into his hand. "Could you deliver this for me, I don't know who it goes to."

"Of course." He takes the note, pushing off from the door. "Thank you for your help. I'm sorry, again. My mind just…" he waves his fingers in the air.

She studies him for a moment. "There is nothing to apologize for." Her smile is shy. "I'm glad I could help. It's scary sometimes, being alone in the world."

"Yes, but you are not alone."

Her eyes meet his.

Percy swallows. "Well, I should inform Frost about my, uh, brain. And deliver this." He steps back, awkward, one of his boughs scraping the frame.

"Take care, Percy."

He raises one hand in the air, unsure if he can speak. Stuffing the paper in his pocket, he heads to the gardens, craving air. The sunlamp room might be quieter but he cannot stand the electricity today. The doors bang open and he half stumbles to a bench, his chest tight.

Divine Hum. Her words, not his. Healing voices and repairing damage. And yet...
Percy buries his head in his hands. Does he only work here to repay what he has done?

The question burns in his mind, agony until he gives it an answer.
No, because he is not built on grief and past sins.
His eyes burn and tears escape. The letter this morning, the writing...they belonged to his brother, once upon a time. The brown eyes that matched his own, the dimpled grin. That's gone now. His brother is gone.

When his breath is easy and the tears have subsided, Percy pulls the note from his pocket, unfolding the seam.

Perhaps the Divine Hum has not forgotten him. Perhaps there is healing waiting for him, too.

There, written in perfect script, are the words *Dear Stranger in the Window.*

The

WOMAN

on the MOON

v.

Days pass.

I pull at words, but they tug me apart.
Untangling my seams and rewriting my
history.
I seek healing from them,
but they condemn my sins, forcing me to look
inward. I am buried in a sea of words, but
have no place to land, no place to give them.
Are you the same?
Do you drown on the inside as I do,
words commanding your head?

Forever-

Daughter of the Seventh Song

Dear Seventh,

Do I drown in words? No.
Words are wind under my broken feathers.
Lifting me from my roots,
tugging me toward the sun.
Words are freedom and peace and insanity and
clarity and truth and lies.
Sometimes words are lies.

They are a light in the darkness, a rapid blinding
force. They are gentle like flowers and
strong like tides and storms.

Words are a gateway to the soul.

They are pure art, connecting the past, present,
and future. Perhaps words are the strings
that formed the world.

Words and sound.

Sincerely yours,

The Stranger in the Window

Dearest Stranger,

How often you speak of sunlight, you must be a child of earth and sky. Your compassion is obvious, and the best part of you. Though I do not know you, somehow in your words I see there has been hurt. One loving as deeply as you must know pain, down to your bones.

I pray you heal from the inside out.

Do not let this hurt twist you into something unrecognizable to love. Be unrecognizable to your pain.

I am a child of long train rides and dark nights. The stars are reflected in me. I try to grow fruit from my scars, to bear goodness from my pain, but only end up revealing old wounds as new ground is spun to face the sun.

There are still things I am trying desperately to heal within me, reaching for the sun with claws instead of kind words.

I fear I will always be storm clouds and moonless nights. I fear I will always be lost between the dark of stars.

Forever-

Daughter of the Seventh Song

Dear Seventh,

The earth is my home, my life and roots. The sky my compassion, my breath and song. If I am light and you are darkness, I wish we had met sooner, for I would have shone my shattered, glimmering pieces of sunlight into your mind, you would pretend they were stars, guiding you home. You would wake from a long dream and know that this light shines for you, too.

You cannot force healing, only pray for the light to break your storm and raise the dawn. You cannot force sunlight to bloom, and I cannot push you into its warm grasp.

I will wait with you, though.

Remind you when your eyes are closed to lean into its warmth. I can show you deep parts of the earth, waiting for your growth, but I cannot force you to grow. I can reveal to you the pure waters of life, but I cannot make you drink.

Healing is not healing if you do not choose it. I offer sunlight, spaces in the earth for your roots, shower rain upon you. I do not wish to touch your healing; my hands are not pure. Let the Divine be the One you reach out for.

Let my words be seeds, settling thoughts in your brain.

Sometimes…if I am honest, I close my eyes to the darkness. Focus on only light. I cannot remember

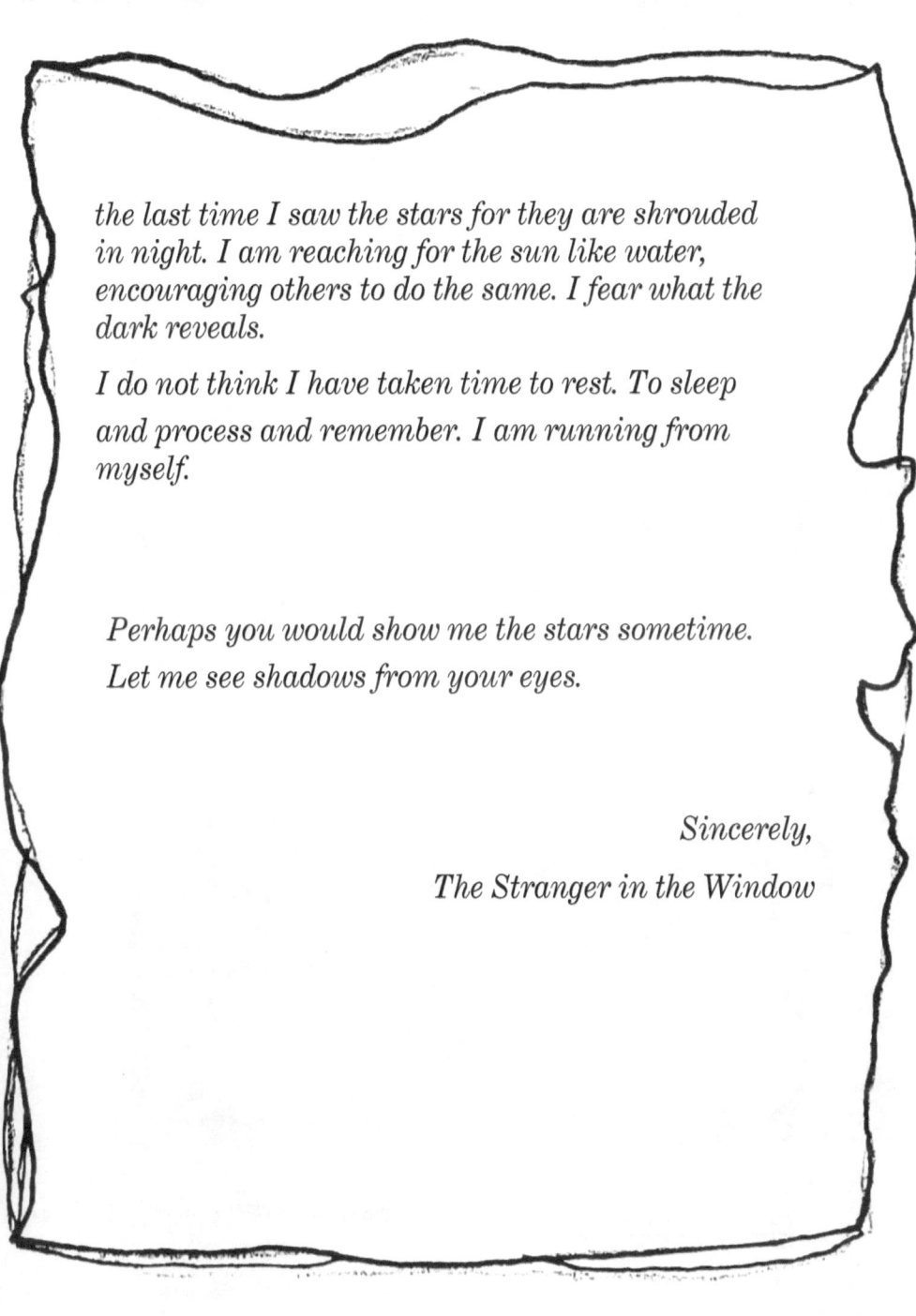

the last time I saw the stars for they are shrouded in night. I am reaching for the sun like water, encouraging others to do the same. I fear what the dark reveals.

I do not think I have taken time to rest. To sleep and process and remember. I am running from myself.

Perhaps you would show me the stars sometime. Let me see shadows from your eyes.

Sincerely,

The Stranger in the Window

Weeks go by.

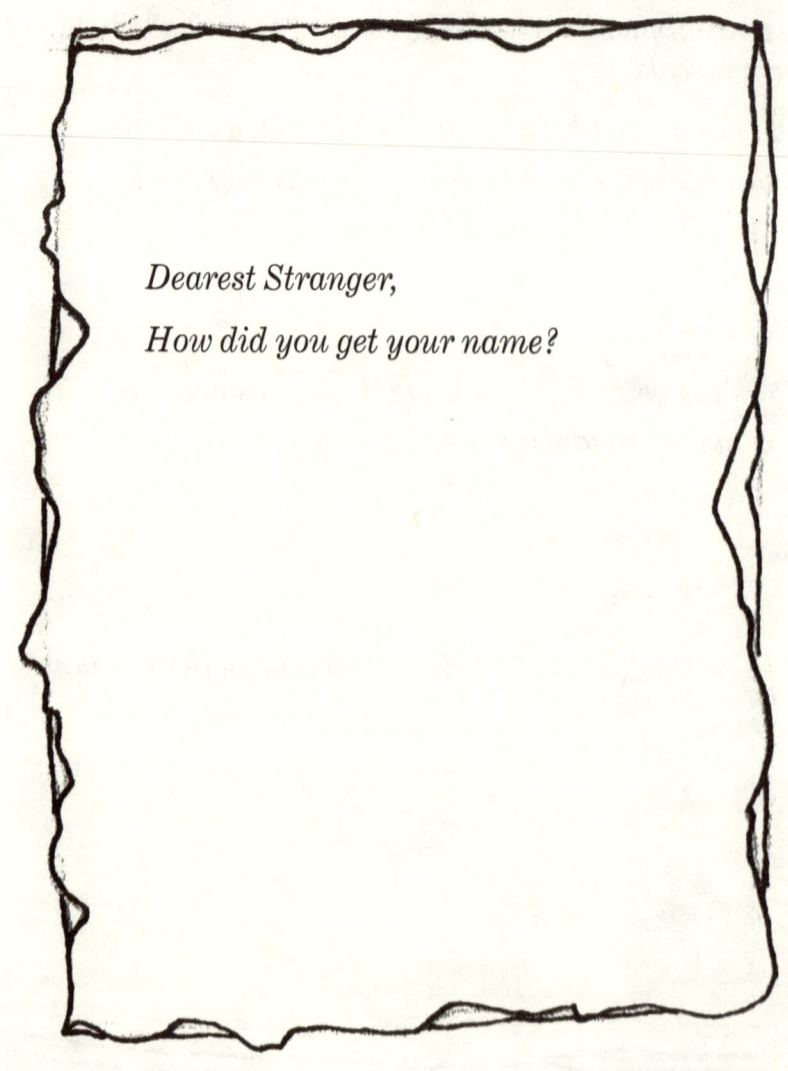

Dearest Stranger,

How did you get your name?

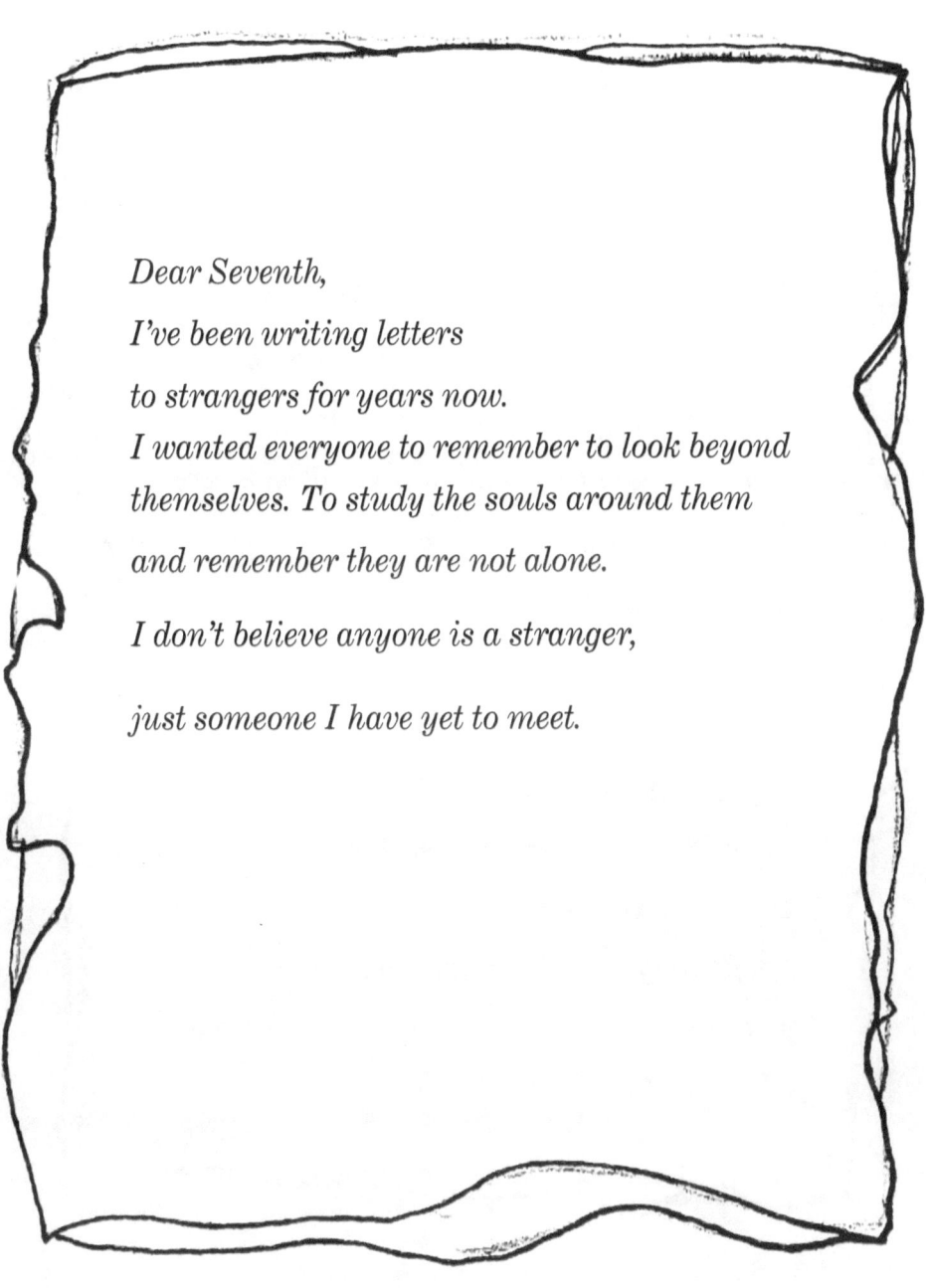

Dear Seventh,

I've been writing letters

to strangers for years now.
I wanted everyone to remember to look beyond
themselves. To study the souls around them

and remember they are not alone.

I don't believe anyone is a stranger,

just someone I have yet to meet.

Dearest Stranger,

I wish I could believe things like that.

All my life there have only been strangers,

and the close, select few.

But even they I have no names for now.

I take your words to heart.

Remind myself I am not alone,

neither are you.

I know not many believe in the Divine Hum

in these modern days.

I would not be alive without the

Divine's soft touch.

I definitely would not be speaking to

you now.

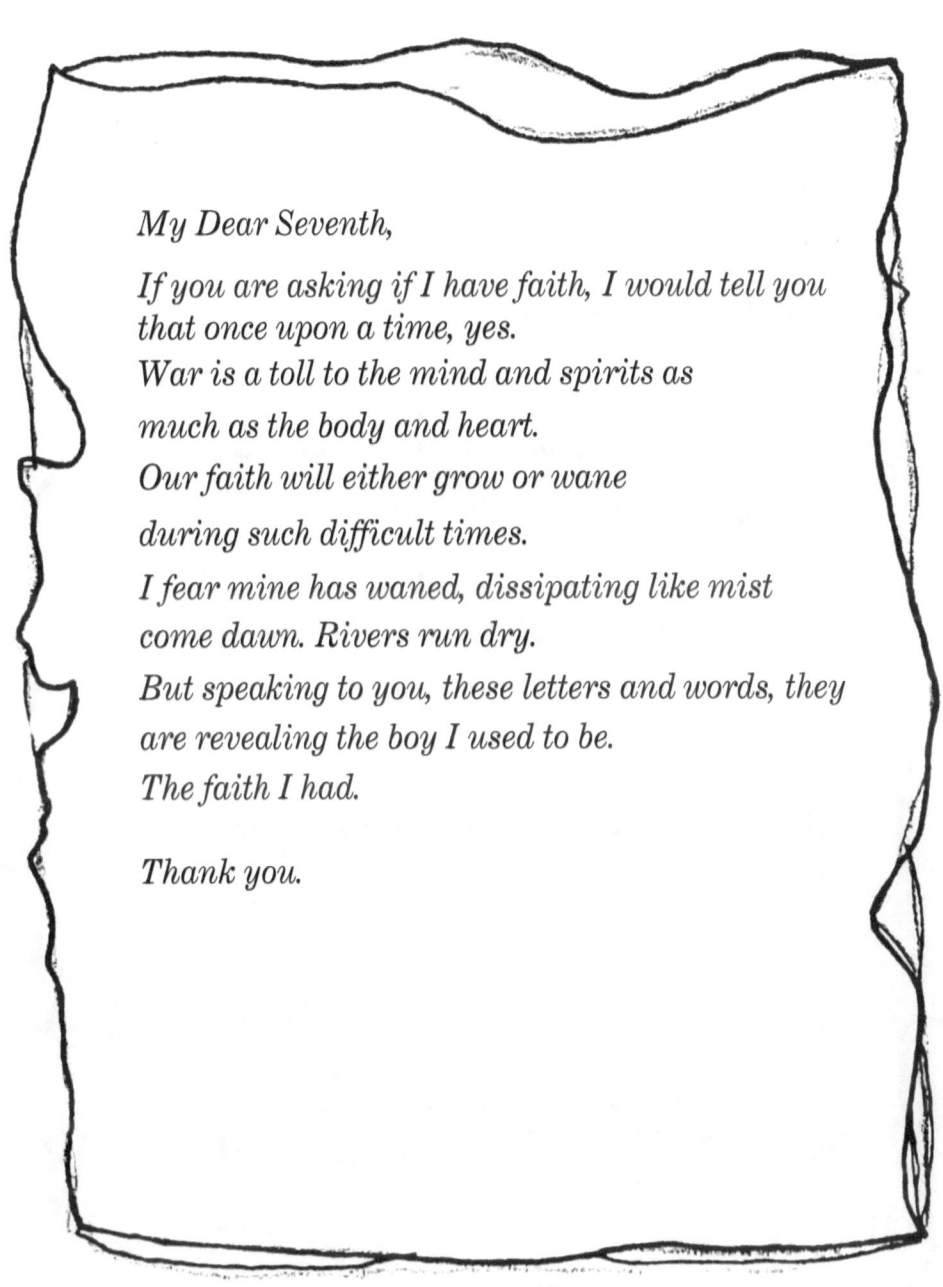

My Dear Seventh,

*If you are asking if I have faith, I would tell you
that once upon a time, yes.
War is a toll to the mind and spirits as
much as the body and heart.
Our faith will either grow or wane
during such difficult times.
I fear mine has waned, dissipating like mist
come dawn. Rivers run dry.
But speaking to you, these letters and words, they
are revealing the boy I used to be.
The faith I had.*

Thank you.

Darling Stranger,

Forever I would write to you, if it meant I
was lifting your beautiful spirit.

Your encouragement for others blooms from you,
but you must remember to water and feed yourself.
An empty garden can give to no one.

I feel as if my faith comes and goes like the tide,
though each day is a little stronger. I believe I have
you to thank for that as well. My spirits have been
lifted greatly by our correspondence.

Do you live in Central Ulna? I would love to meet
you.

Forever yours-

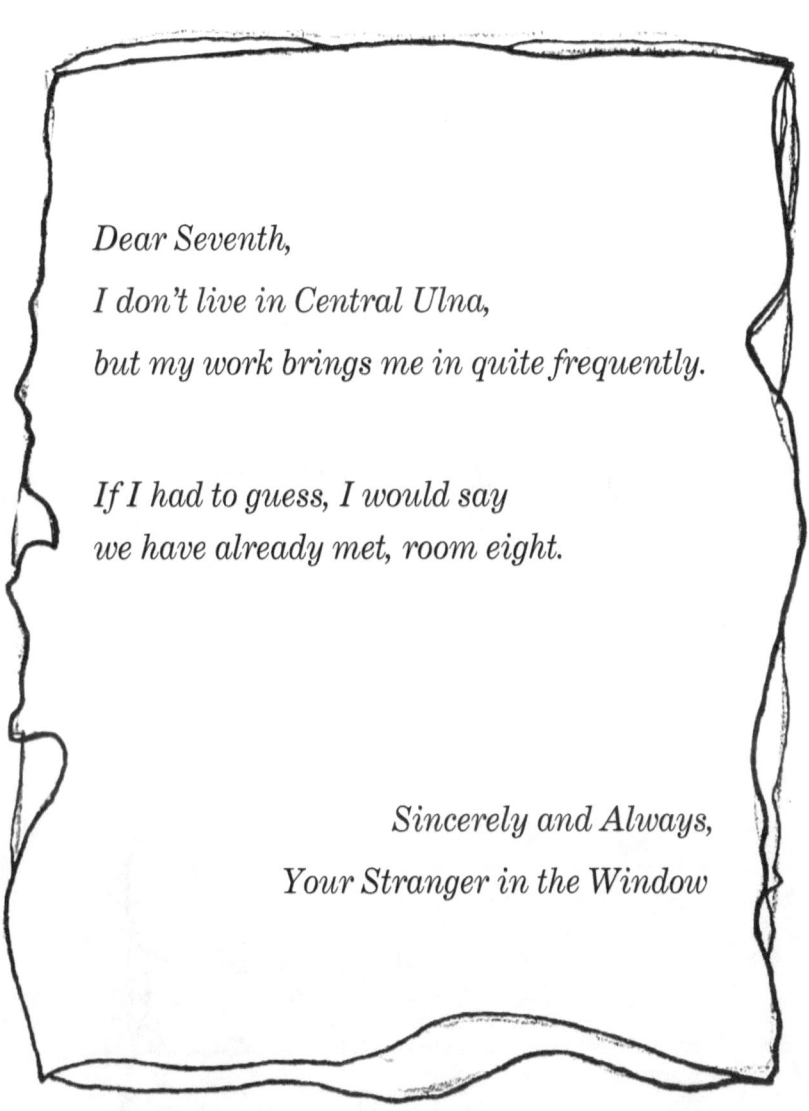

Dear Seventh,

I don't live in Central Ulna,

but my work brings me in quite frequently.

If I had to guess, I would say
we have already met, room eight.

Sincerely and Always,
Your Stranger in the Window

Time is nothing to them.

My dear Percy,

I knew it was you.

My soul found yours in words and

I was blessed enough to be given

a face to match.

Somehow,

I always knew it was you.

-Always Alyce

Tell me a story, Percy.
Please.

The Woman on the Moon

There once was a woman on the moon. Her skin was dusty and pale and grey as storm clouds and the underbelly of birds.

To fill the loneliness, she wrote letters, letting them flutter down to earth. Page after page after page came across the heavenly sea to rest on earth's shore.

A boy read the words, felt them inside. Taking up a pen, he wrote in return, sending them out to the sea in hopes they would reach her.

Tomes and chronicles and libraries could have been filled with the letters passed between the two

Ages passed. The love burning in the boy's chest became an immortal flame, turning his skin to bark, his hands boughs and roots, his feet become the deep foundation of earth's shore.

"If I had wings, I would soar to you. If I was Earth Herself, I would spin ever closer to you. Would you come to me, so I might meet you."

"I will come. I will come and spin in your arms! Tell me your name, so I might know you when I land. I am Nadala."

"Nadala. Nadala. Nadala. How I long to say your name, caress your face. I am Lor. I am waiting for you."

Nadala worked night and day, forming a bridge from the letters they had written. Ink and curled pages spiraled down from the moon, dipping into the heavenly sea.

"I am coming. Soon I will be with you. Wait for me." Nadala sends one last letter from her home, watching the wind take place it into her love's hand. Nadala places one foot on the bridge, her structure holding secure. Another step. Another. Soon she is running from the ecstasy of having someone to run to. She takes no heed of the way her bridge tilts and turns beneath her, not until her next steps land in the air and for a moment she is flying...then she falls.

As if her words were wings, they fall with her, landing in the heavenly sea with the force of a hurricane. Papers float atop the waves, but Nadala sinks to the bottom of the sea.

"My love, are you near? Many nights it has been, and I cannot see your light upon the moon. The world is dark without you." Lor writes, pressing leafy lips to his message.

Again and again he writes unread letters to his love. Praying she is near, that someday she will hear him.

His words float out on lazy tides or roar and plunge with the waves and storms, reaching the heavenly sea and riding up to the moon. So many

*letters does he write, that soon the moon is
cluttered with pages and ink and lost words.*

Nadala has not returned.

*"What am I to do?" Lor cries out to the air and
winds and earth. "Have I lost her forever?"*

*"We have seen her," the winds reply. "She fell
from the sky, landing in the sea."*

*Lor cries harder, curling in on himself. "I am
rooted and a creature of the sun. I cannot go
beneath the waves to search for her."*

*"We will go, we will search, we might be able to
reach her." The tides call, lifting and falling, the
breath of a giant.*

*"Go, and search for her then." Lor tells the sea. It
takes many days and nights, spinning into years
and then centuries. Lor's tears form around him as
the sea around the earth, he curls into himself, salt
mingling out to the pure heavenly sea.*

*Lor bows his head, giving his tears to the sun,
who grants him the seeds of moon flowers. Lor
plants the flowers within himself, blooming tiny
white petals, pointing to the four winds.*

*"As wide as the earth is, I cross it to meet you."
He sets a petal in the water.*

*"As deep as the sea, I swim to find you." Another
flower.*

"As high as the skies, I grow to see you.

As inky as the moon, I write to your soul.

As warm as the sun, I burn for you, granting you life with my love.

As flowers bloom only once, I will love only once. Only you."

Each word, each letter, each tear fallen, Lor places a white flower into the sea. They gather and spin and ride away from him, clustered like the moon on the sea's surface.

"As long as I have already waited, I would add another thousand years if it means it is you I am waiting for." Lor whispers, wind taking his words, giving them to the waves. Waves taking his words, giving them to the tides. Tides taking his words, carrying them deep into the sea.

Nadala has forgotten her name. Her voice. Her home. Her love. She remembers only the terror of her fall. The pain of her crash.

I cannot move from this place, she thinks, for the pain will only follow me.

"You would poison the sea with your thoughts?" The tides ask her.

"No. I wish to be free, but I am afraid." She replies.

"It is this fear which is the prison. You must remember the light." The tides caress her cheeks, giving her a name and a jumble of teary words.

"Such passion." She gasps at the words from a voice she should know. Life flooding her arteries, panic circled out through her veins.

"Hope awaits you on the surface. He will wait forever for you."

"I'm not ready. I'm- I'm still afraid. What if this pain returns? What if this is a lie and there is only darkness awaiting me? What if I don't have the strength to return this love?"

"There will always be fear in this darkness, but Hope waits for you in eternal light, extending his hand. He will always extend his hand to you. He will always wait; his love is true. His love is safe."

Nadala rises, slowly, walking through the darkness of the sea floor. The moon is above her, white and delicate through the water.

Nadala tucks a tiny, white flower behind her ear.

With each step she rises a little higher, takes in a little more light, until she glows like the sun.

"There is no light here, why do I shimmer so?"

"It is the salt of Hope's tears; they have formed you into something new amid the pressure you faced."

Nadala rises to the surface of the world a diamond.

Lor waits for her, frozen in place along the shore. Nadala is slow to walk to him, sunlight casting rainbows within her, a halo of color atop the pale sands.

She presses lips to his, breaking his spell of loneliness.

"Nadala." He breathes, and the sound is perfect. Her name does not contain the darkness she endured, or the pain waiting caused him. The sound is pure.

"Lor." His name is lightning within her, burning through her vascular system like air on fire in her veins.

"I have fallen so I could love you." She says. "I have risen so I could know you."

vi.

Percy waits in the shadow of Alyce's voice. Poetry
and short stories fall from her lips like water and
starlight. Sunlight bathes room four in gold.
Mabel is smiling, leaning back in the light; Alyce
sits in the darkness of the room, reading softly.

He raps the door once, poking his head in,
breaking the afternoon peace.

Alyce smiles at him, her face flushing slightly. He
cannot help his own grin.

"Hi, Miss Mabel, it's Percy." He taps her wrist
with two fingers, letting her know where he is. She
holds out her hand to him, letting him check her
pulse, flash a light in her eyes, he check for possible
swelling along her cranial lobe with his gentle fingers.

"How are you feeling?" He steps back, his eyes
sliding unintentionally to Alyce.

"Oh, I feel fine. Wonderful." Mabel moves her
head to Alyce's direction, her words heartfelt.
"Thank you."

"I'm glad." Alyce smiles tiredly, even though Mabel cannot see her expression. She gathers papers and loose pens, scribbling poems for Mabel and leaving them for her at the bedside with a touch and a soft word.

Alyce brushes past Percy, the sleeve of her hospital gown touching his arm.

His eyes follow her from the room, then turn back to Mabel, finishing his assessment. "Now, I don't have total say, head Doctor Rossi will be the one to determine , but I've heard you'll be discharged soon."

Mabel's face lights up. She presses warm, brown hands to her cheeks.

"My husband knows?"

"Yes. He is aware and very excited. I'll leave you now, Rossi will be stopping by with discharge papers."

"Thank you." Mabel sighs, falling back onto her pillows.

Percy nods, "of course." He gives a small smile and leaves with a touch to her wrist.

Alyce is waiting in the hall for him.

"Going to the gardens?" He raises a brow at her.

Alyce shakes her head; Percy doesn't push that she must need light of *some kind*. Her dark face pale. Half moons mar her eyes. She's exhausted. Still she refuses Afiya and electric sunlamps. Healing will take longer for her. Percy wonders if she intentionally wanted to stay.

"It's good you're up and walking more. How are you feeling?"

"Well enough. I already have Jasmine checking up on me, I don't need another nurse." She smiles cheekily, teasing.

Percy puts his hands up. "Excuse me for doing my job." But he's smiling too. Oh Earth, Alyce is the sun in Etz form. Tiny boughs wrap her head, a silent diadem of life.

"I'm sorry, but I don't have much time today. Can I reschedule our chat for tomorrow?"
Alyce nods, slightly crestfallen.

Percy's heart pinches. He will miss meeting under the large window overlooking the gardens. Exchanging poems and reading softly to each other as easy as breathing.

Their letters have grown and become a force of their own, ocean tides and hurricanes. Forces of life trapped in ink and thoughts.

It's odd, almost, seeing each other in person after so many raw thoughts have been laid bare in their hands.

Alyce coughs suddenly, burying her mouth in the crook of her arm.

"Oh, that doesn't sound good." Percy reaches to place a supportive hand on her back, but she finches away from him. His hand hesitates in the air, then he removes the thermometer from his pocket, holding it to her forehead.

He bites a curse on his tongue.

"You're burning up. Alyce, how long have you been sick?"

She shrugs, holding her companiable papers to her chest.

Percy gestures down the hall, forcing her to walk into her room. She sits on the bed, and Percy wets a cloth, placing it on the back of her neck.

"I'll send Jasmine in, I need to check on room seven's meds. I'll be right back."

She nods wearily, holding the cool cloth to the base of her skull.

Percy gives her a warning look. "Don't leave."

"I won't."

He waits for a moment, her face weary. Dark circles mar her eyes, skin flushed. She sways on the bed.

"Here." Percy digs is his pocket, handing her a vial of soft yellow light. "It's lavender flavored."

Alyce appears as if he has gone mad.

"Afiya. Condensed light. Don't drink it all in one place." He smiles, but she doesn't get the joke.

"Seriously, I'll be right back."

Part of him aches to place a hand on her cheek, press lips to her forehead. He holds himself back; it takes more strength than he thought it should.

Percy knocks on room seven's door. A curtsy considering the patient still hasn't woken.

"Coming in." Percy calls softly, entering the dim room. He opens the curtains, fixes the bedsheets and checks vitals.

"Heartrate a little elevated today." Percy notes the numbers with a mark on the wall chart.

A small tap. The sound of a finger raised and dropped.

Percy eyes the sleeping boy, his marred face. Scar tissue riddles across his nose, cheeks and left temple, streaking down his neck like veins.

Percy knew more than he wanted to of wounds from fire. These scars were too old to be from the war. The boughs twisting up from his head are almost regal, though ashen with illness. A sunlamp waits in the corner, a daily dose of light still needed. Percy sighs, flipping the switch. He misses the calming buzz of the ion lights compared to the King's new electricity, humming a distorted song.

Meds are good. He prepares a syringe for pain, made from willow bark, turmeric, and labradorite.

The boy flinches on the bed, fingers twitching. Percy freezes. Hands shaking, he sets down the drugs, mixing like a thunderstorm inside the glass.

"Hello, can you hear me?" Percy places two fingers on the boy's wrist. He winces, Percy recoils his hand.

"W-Wa-ter." The boy struggles to swallow. "Water." Voice raspy, as if he has been screaming. Percy fetches him a glass, pressing the edge to his lips, proping him carefully on pillows. The boy sips cautiously, then swallows mouthfuls at a time.

"Whao, drinking too much will make you sick." Percy pulls the cup away.

Sated and stomach gurgling, the boy leans back against his bed.

"Where am I?" One eye slits open, a bloodshot blue orb landing on Percy.

"Halo Hospital, sir. You've been receiving treatments for a coma. It says here…" Percy flips through the pages of daily charting, finding the date of admission. "You've been here for…nine weeks. Do you have any pain as we speak?"

The boy groans, rolling himself upright, Percy scurrying to assist. "Nothing you can help with." He says with a moan, wiggling his arm from Percy's grip. "Does my father know I'm here?"

"Your father?"

The boy arches a regal brow, eyes fluttering close. "Yes. Usis, King of Ulna. Does he know where I am?"

Percy's stomach drops. The scarred, unrecognizable face. The Prince always wore a mask, meaning these scars were not from the war, as the hospital staff thought, but long before that.

"You are Prince Raedyn." Percy squeezes the words from his throat, locking his knees to stay in place.

"Unfortunately." The boy sighs, leaning back in the bed. "Could you turn out the lights? I don't like the electricity. The frequency makes me ache."

Percy flicks off the sunlamp with trembling fingers, leaving him and the crown Prince of Ulna in darkness.

The Prince is moved to a secure wing of the hospital. Percy paces the hall, running a trembling hand through his dull, golden hair.

"Percy, here." Frost hands him a portable sun lamp. "You need to rest."

"Thanks." Percy takes the round lamp, but doesn't turn it on, reminded of the Prince's slurred words. The odd, haunting frequency.

The King's electricity is like oil in the blood. Sluggish and chaining.

"You've alerted the authorities?" Percy asks, fingers interlocking and breaking apart.

"The King has been summoned. He claims to be coming." Frost's voice takes a condemning tilt. "His own son." Frost shakes his head, muttering. "If we had known... why did no one come looking for him?"

"I don't know. And the Prince's face..." Percy lowers his voice. "Something isn't right." He sets the sunlamp on the floor, watching it pulse with frequency in his mind's eye. There is no color, the hues associated with all sounds and vibrations. There is no *life*. This is an empty song, stealing instead of giving.

Percy buries his face, then rises. "I'll take first watch tonight."

Frost catches sight of his watch, rubs the back of his neck and sighs. "I'll let Rossi know. We're locking hospital doors tonight. No one in or out after eight."

Percy nods, turning the knob and entering Prince Rae's room.

The boy is asleep, eyes scrunched as if trapped in a nightmare. Percy paces softly, then settles down in the lone chair. He remembers Alyce's voice coming from the Prince's bedside. Everyday she has read to Prince Rae, Mabel, himself even, when he stood outside the door, loving the way poetry fell from her lips like water.

Percy eyes the Prince's scarred, ruined face. Who would do this to a child? Force him to cover his face, hiding an ugly scar this whole time.

Exhausted on multiple levels, Percy crosses his arms, perhaps trying to hide this large, feeling side of himself. He never mastered being an emotionless soldier.

Percy is the sea, tossing and always unsure if he is rising or falling. He has been falling for too long now, forcing himself onward, frightened the crashing impact might shatter bones. Shatter the foundation of this shield he built around himself.

He has never been emotionless, not even after he'd done the unthinkable. He squeezes his eyes shut, his brother's face flashing in and out of his vision. What had they fought for? *Died* for? A rumor of peace treaties? Possible alignment with the same country who pushed against the Sun King's own peace offerings, thus leaving Usis to strike war? Is that what started all this, the ruined faces of royals and brothers who would never smile again, because someone was offended?

Percy folds into himself, feeling small. He watches Rae's chest fall and rise in labored breaths until the moon is high, and then till the sun starts to wake.

vii.

Alyce is spinning, unstoppable as the Earth around the sun. Or perhaps she is the sun, earth orbiting her. This room, these hospital walls, this city, they circle around her.

"I am the sun." She whispers, fevered. She fingers Percy's Afiya vial, the yellow light a fire on her skin. Something has happened outside, but her body is shaking so bad, she doesn't dare move from the bed.

Percy does not return. Neither does Jasmine. There are voices, harsh tones and frantic shoes pounding the tiled flooring.

Alyce curls on her side, holding her throbbing, fevered head.

Minutes then hours, time is nothing but a reminder of the large, blaring sun, then the full moon over the hospital gardens, glowing at her from on high. Alyce finally falls into sleep, Percy's vial of Afiya clutched in her hand. She doesn't drink.

Something wakes her. Footsteps in the hall, or the knock on the door; there is too much noise. Alyce alerts herself to the world with a groan. Jasmine flicks a light in her eyes, checks her temperature, heart rate and blood pressure.

"How long have you been like this?" She removes the now heated cloth from Alyce's neck, replacing it with a cool one.

"I don't know." Alyce groans, feeling the loose branches shift on her head as she curls deeper into herself.

Jasmine removes the sheets, Alyce flinches. "We need to get your fever down."

Jasmine works in a daze Alyce tries to wake from. She pulls herself upright on trembling arms, something falling from her head. Nothing matters anymore. Nothing that cannot be fixed with more sleep.

Bleary eyes scan the bed and Alyce stares in horror at the limp roots, her failed pass at appearing Etz, dislodged from her curls.

Jasmine's face is expressionless, lavender eyes widening as Alyce lifts the thin roots.

"I- I can explain."

Jasmine shakes her head, stepping back. "I'm- I'm sorry." She looks over Alyce's ash dark skin, her grey eyes, the nurses face slipping toward horror.

Jasmine turns from her, and Alyce grips her sheets, the soldier in her preparing to run.

"I will finish your treatment." Her voice is ice. "Because I am a healer." She doesn't turn to her. "Then you need to go. One of your people will be arriving with the King today, I will make sure they know you are here."

Jasmine casts her a smile, like she is doing her a favor, not throwing her to the wolves she ran from.

Alyce grips down on her panic, Percy's bottle biting into her skin. Good. She needs to wake up. "I didn't ask to be admitted. I was brought here unconsciously. Your doctor's treated my wounds, and you have housed and cared for me. I didn't ask for that." She cannot keep the injustice from her voice, her fever making her reckless.

Jasmine tightens her lips. "And I didn't ask for a war that killed my family. Your people did when you refused our King."

"Yes, but not me specifically. Are we going to place mass blame, or will you hunt down the names of whoever caused you such harm?"

Jasmine shutters. Alyce feels guilt, hot red spite, like a shot through her chest.

"Everyone is guilty of something." Jasmine says softly. "Who am I to say one guilt is greater than another. I do not know the things you have done."

Her words douse the growing anger in Alyce.

Jasmine places meds for fever on Alyce's small table.

"I'll alert the King now." Her voice is so gentle, as if she were fetching a loved one. "He'll know where you belong."

"Thank you." It's all she can choak out, praying her anxiety is invisible. Then the door closes and Jasmine is gone. Alyce shoots to her feet, stumbling for a moment. She takes the meds, swallowing them like an acid. She needs all the strength she can get. There's a wing near the back of the hospital that has laid empty, she'll leave through there, avoid being spotted as much as possible. She doesn't know how many people Jasmine will tell before she's out of time.

She dresses quickly, her breath labored and hot, her body shaking. Her old clothes are here, black pants the style her father always wore, a coat depicting her station and rank embroidered on the sleeve in bloodied gold thread. It will mark her as someone her father wanted her to be. It will mark her as a royal soldier of Radius. Whoever found her knew what she was, chose to bring her to this hospital. Perhaps there are larger minds at play.

Alyce turns the coat inside out.

Her steps are quick and barefooted. She carries only Percy's vial in her pocket and stuffs the overflowing little book into her coat. She's still wearing the hospital gown underneath and looks slightly ridiculous with her wild hair, flushed, fevered cheeks and an old army uniform. She rounds one corner, slowing when she passes an unfamiliar nurse. She gives the young girl a smile.

Two more long halls prove to be empty and Alyce pushes her shoulder against a large set of doors, slipping between them and wincing when they shut with a groan.

This must be the empty wing. She runs now, bare foot and almost silent. Breath hot and labored, lungs working overtime. Almost there-

She slows, skidding into a curving wall when voices pierce her fog.
She tilts her head around the curve, spotting a smattering of figures in everything from regal uniforms, soldiers' garb, officials and doctors and nurses.

Panic rips claws around her throat when the Sun King himself shifts in their midst, beside a man she knows all too well.

King Silver's ambassador of peace stands next to the Sun king with an important expression on his face, and beside him...

Alyce swallows, wishing she could remember her father from before the war, when his smiles were larger than the moon and his laugh quick. Now his face is chipped and expressionless. Jaal shifts beside Radius's ambassador, his stiff stance enough to send Alyce's heart racing.

He cannot find her!

She turns, intending to run the opposite way, when the Sun King's next words send chills down her nerves.

"Bring me the one who found my son."

Was Prince Rae here?! This entire time?!

Alyce presses herself into the wall, daring to creep closer. Just an inch.

There's a shuffle of feet, then a figure steps forward from the outskirts. Standing as far from King Usis as he possibly can, is Percy.

Alyce's heart starts to ache without warning, forcing her to breathe.

His hands are trembling. Alyce squeezes her own.

"I must thank you for the finding of my son." The King says, voice booming, covering the edge tinted in his words.

"Come, let me bless you with light." He holds out his hand to Percy, heat radiating from curled fingers.

Alyce can remember the day Usis became King, anointed because light poured from him. Even now his eyes are holding a gentle glow, one Alyce knows could burn down cities if it became strong enough. *Has* burnt down cities. She swallows, her throat unbearably dry.

Percy hesitates, then steps forward even as Alyce internally yells at him to run. Of course, you could not refuse a gift from the King.

"I'm afraid I must decline, your majesty. I'm all full at the moment."

A few scattered laughs. The King gives a tight smile. "Another time. I must ask you remain guarded until I can thank you properly." He snaps, a guard steps forward, bows, extending her fisted hands to the king, then to Percy.

"Really, I don't need a guard-"

"Twice you refuse me." The King tuts. Dead silence. "All is well," he waves a jeweled hand. "I will find a way to repay." The last word bares a threat, sharp and pointed. Percy is trembling now, visibly and body wide. An energy of grief and fear vibrating through his form.

"I must see my son." The King turns toward the door, his assembly following him into the dark room, bringing light the King gently radiates.

Percy is left alone in the hall. He turns toward Alyce, as if sensing she is there.

Alyce stumbles back. She cannot let him see her in army clothing and on the run. Alyce does not know what he will do. Yet she trusts him.

She digs paper from her book, tearing through words they have shared.

This could be the most foolish thing in her life,
speaking to him in this way when her freedom is so close.
Alyce doesn't base her life choices off of logic, though; it
is faith running through her now.

Writing a quick note, she slides it along the floor,
satisfied when it lands near his feet. She doesn't
stay to see him read it, to see if he will even lift her
words from the floor. She only continues to the exit,
footsteps hurried, thunder beneath her. Throwing
doors open into a bright, burning afternoon, she
sucks in a breath and runs.

viii.

Percy lifts the note with trembling hands, reading the swift and messy words.

> *Percy,*
>
> *I need to leave Central Ulna and don't know how I will find you again. I don't mean to frighten you-*

Percy doesn't read the rest of the words, only runs. Through halls and out doors. Pounding along the sidewalks and crossing streets as if he could fly.

He reaches the train station, the only major transportation in Ulna. He scans the crowd, disappointment blooms in his chest. She could already be on a train, traveling far from him, or perhaps she is here in the masses, watching him or hiding herself.

What would have made her so afraid she couldn't wait to be discharged? And her fever- Percy slaps a hand on his forehead.

She's ill, wounded, alone, and probably barefoot. Percy slumps against a main entrance post, scanning every face, searching eyes and skin color.

None match her moonlit eyes and midnight skin. Her strong energy, churning beneath the surface of her skin, like a thunderstorm waiting to break.

His head hits the pole, cool against his back and neck. He hasn't stopped shaking. Crimson orbs are seared into his vision, charred skin and last screams. He cannot remove Rae's ruined face from his mind, the heat radiating from Usis' grip. Something is wrong in the capital.

Percy cannot breathe, and pushes his head between his knees, trying to regain thinking capabilities. Time becomes a blur and he's stopped searching faces, too dizzy to move.

A hand on his shoulder startles him, brings tears to his eyes as he is transported back to a time any contact meant danger. Sol's dark, green-grey orbs meet his, night blooms and grows and Percy realizes he has been here for hours.

"I've come to take you home, son." Sol helps him to his feet, steadying him. Though the Alom man is two feet shorter than he, Sol's strength radiates, pushing Percy to his feet.

"I'm waiting for- I needed-" Percy gasps, anxiety bright in his chest and he closes his eyes against its light.

Sol guides him toward the waiting train, Percy fights against him, loosening his grip.

"Wait. Wait." He pulls a used medical paper from his coat, writing with shaking hands.

He draws a tiny, four-pointed flower on the folded page, praying she remembers what it means as he sticks it to the post with used tape.

Then he lets Sol draw him from the massing crowds and onto the train. They ride home in silence.

"This is the fourteenth anxiety attack since you began working there. It's not good for you. I know you feel guilt over the war and your part in it, but everyone is guilty of something, and you cannot work yourself, with no pay, into the ground over someone you used to be." Sol lectures him, lovingly, while Percy stares into a cup of warm Afiya. Purple and ink dark red mix in a glittering haze, grounding and renewing. He sips.

"I mean, I *'used to be someone'*, and you don't see me working in every goodytooshoos corporation to 'do good.'" Sol waves his fingers in the air.

"That's not my intention and that is *not* how you use that phrase."

"Whatever." Sol waves a hand. "This doesn't bring your brother back. This doesn't fix what broke." His voice softens, just a touch. "The world broke, alright? You are not the one who's meant to fix it." Sol considers him, labradorite orbs scanning weary eyes and pale skin. Percy's shoulders bowed over his cup, fingers fighting to relax.

"I'm writing your boss; you're taking some time off."

"Sol, I cannot-"

Sol gives him a dark look. "Yes, you can. You just saved the Prince's life, and the kingdom, you'll do what you like."

Percy doesn't respond.

"You are going to give yourself time to heal. Really heal." Sol presses. "Verses working yourself to the bone in order to forget and feel forgiven."

Percy starts to protest. That wasn't why he worked at Halo. Not entirely. He takes another swig, the mixture bringing clarity and peace simultaneously.

"This hasn't been working, Percy. You need time. Your mind needs time. Your soul has been aching and weary and cannot be forced any further. Trust me." He says softly. Sol places a hand on his. "I can see you, even when you can't. You don't need a band aid job, you need to give yourself grace and move on. Move forward."

Percy nods, weary. His shaking has stopped, his mind clearing of anxiety. His heart is still a frantic drum within him.

"I want to bring peace." He says softly. Sol sits with a sigh beside him.

"I know."

"I wanted to make a difference and yes, in the beginning, I thought that meant war."

"You knew it wasn't the war; you followed your brother. In life and in death you follow him, but now it is time to change the course of the river, you cannot survive in this muck."

"I tried to be emotionless, like they taught us." He continues, voice hallow. "I never managed it. I fought with more emotion than I've ever felt. So much rage was in my veins...after Ojo died... it was the only thing that kept me moving. What if I lost myself? On the battlefields of death, what if I'm never coming back from that?" His voice cracks, broken glass in his throat.

The tears are hot and Percy is ashamed of them. They splash into his Afiya and burn on his cheeks.

"You are, Percy. You will. And if you don't, I will return to that pit and pull you out of it. You hear me, boy? I'm not letting this get the better of you, you deserve more than that. And if you think less of yourself because you *survived on rage*, don't be. I've never been so glad of anger in my life; it kept you alive. Now I will help you learn to live without it."

"I can't remember the last time I just...felt hope. For the future. Or thought of the future at all. Have I really been living in this daze?"

"I mean," Sol shrugs. "You're cooking could have more focus- what!? I'm kidding." Sol chuckles at his own joke, face going serious with his next words. "No Percy, you are the most alive person I have ever met. And if you feel like your light is failing, then show me, tell me. I will do everything in my power to ignite you again." Sol brightens. "Starting with quitting your job for you."

"Sol, no. What will I do with myself?" Percy groans, pushing back from the table. But he doesn't stand, doesn't protest as Sol writes up a resignation letter, even fixes some of the numbers on the address for him.

"Don't worry, you can finally earn your keep by helping me fix this place up." Sol grins.

Percy lays his head on the table as Sol walks out to the mailbox. Oddly refreshed from crying and pouring broken pieces of him onto the kitchen table, Percy smiles a little. How did he end up with the most perfect friend.

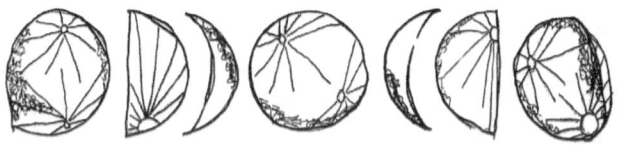

ix.

Alyce runs deep into the night, stopping only when the lights of the train station come into view. She had never been outside the hospital and finding it took embarrassingly long, but necessary. She will slip inside, ride away to some distance city. Away from her father and Radius and wicked Kings.

"Wait, dear one. Wait."

Her steps stumble, the voice ripping through her, gentle and unrelenting as a brook.

She pauses just outside the entrance gates, feeling like Nadala, drawn to the white flower sketched on a slip of paper. She tugs it free.

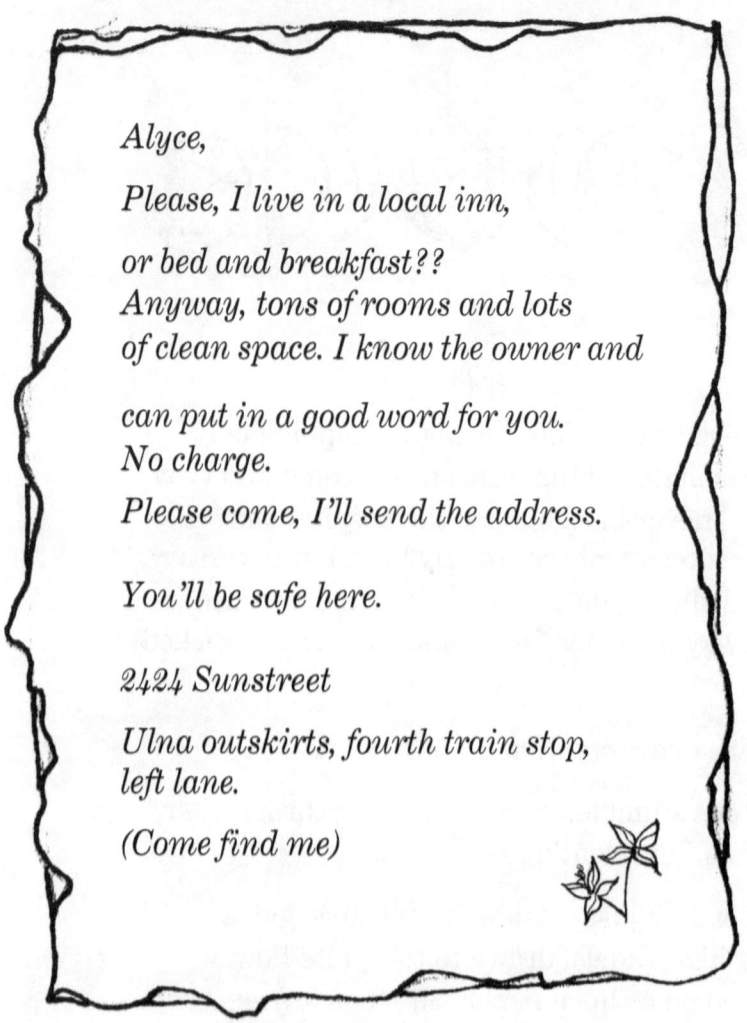

Alyce,

Please, I live in a local inn,

or bed and breakfast??
Anyway, tons of rooms and lots
of clean space. I know the owner and

can put in a good word for you.
No charge.

Please come, I'll send the address.

You'll be safe here.

2424 Sunstreet

Ulna outskirts, fourth train stop,
left lane.

(Come find me)

Two payment chips for the train sit folded within the paper. Alyce could cry.

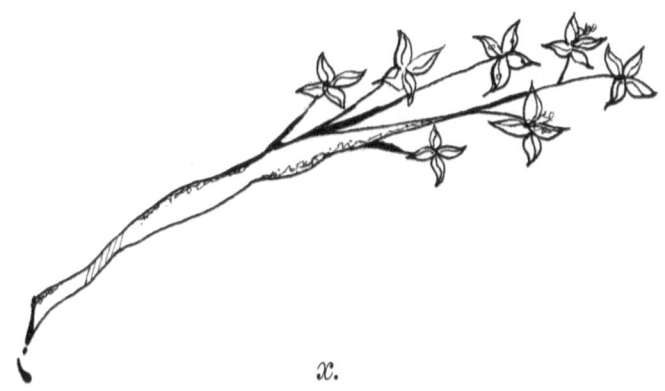

x.

Percy wakes to a pressure in his chest. An urgency. The first light of dawn kisses through the kitchen window, blue and hazy. Stars speckled and distant. A blanket slips from his shoulders, one Sol placed around his form when he insisted on staying awake. So much for that.

Percy stands, runs a hand through his rumpled curls. He stumbles to the counter, leaning against the sink. Glowing bottles of Afiya illuminate the room with tiny halos of yellows and blues and crimsons. He rubs a hand over his chest, tight with worry. The latch on the window is broke, sealed tight. Percy pushes against the glass to no avail. He's too exhausted for this. Sighing, he gives up, padding toward the foyer. He's tempted to check the spare room, adjust the pillows for the umpteenth time. He resists the urge to scrub the floors again.

The front door is unlocked, swinging open on silent hinges. Percy leans against the frame, dawn crawling slowly into the sky, a chill spreading over his arms.

"Sorry I'm late."

Percy jumps as a shadow struggles to rise from the darkness, her trembling hand steadying her as she leans against the wall. Alyce's eyes glow like the moon on his front porch.

Relief pulses through him.

"Or early?" She cocks her head, voice slurring, eyeing his bedraggled clothes.

Dark moons mar her eyes, face pale, cheeks flushed. Her breath curls in the air, a cloud of fevered exhales.

"Alyce." Disbelief fills his voice. He takes a step forward, hesitantly, afraid she will run from him. She doesn't move. Doesn't flinch when he raises a hand to her forehead. His voice softens. "Are you okay?"

She nods wearily. Percy steadies her shoulders, stopping a mere breath from her.

They stand for a moment, the light of the porch illuminating their two worlds, joining warm kitchen light and dark train rides.

Then Sol's voice dips around the corner. "Are you going to let her in, boy?"

"Oh, right." Percy flushes. "Can you walk?"

She doesn't answer, and Percy has one of her arms looped over his shoulder before she can protest. Part of him itches to scoop her into his arms, yet he doesn't want to frighten her.

He shuts the door carefully behind them, afraid she might disappear. Alyce takes in the room, the curved stairs, the narrow hallway leading to the back of the house where Sol lives, the warm light coming from the kitchen.

She leans toward him, whispering, breath hot, "I thought you said this was clean."

Percy's face instantly heats. "Um, well, you see I-"

"Percy, I'm joking." She smiles a little, exhaustion turning it into a grimace.

"Right." Percy prays she cannot feel his heart thudding.

Sol leans over the ion stove in the kitchen. "I hope you like raspberry Afiya." He smiles, turning to greet them. His eyes widen a fraction when Alyce steps into the light, snug in Percy's grip. He gasps as if she is a ghost. Pupils dilating, holding a second of horror before a neutral gaze glasses over him.

"Sol Noli." He introduces, extending a hand Alyce doesn't take. Percy feels her tense, taking a subtle step closer to him.

"Let's eat, yeah?" He grins, trying to dispel the tension. Alyce nods, smiling shyly.

"Are you always up this early?" She asks, the exhaustion evident in her voice. Percy hands her some warm Afiya. She doesn't drink.

Sol gives her a grimacing smile, his left eye twitching. "No. Someone insisted we wait for you, in case you came in the night."

Alyce lifts her eyes to Percy, who looks down, swirling his own drink before taking a long swig.

"You didn't have to go through so much trouble."

"Not at all." Percy interjects loudly. "I almost thought you wouldn't- that you would not come at all." He's fumbling. "I know I gave you the address, but if there is somewhere else you'd rather be-"

"No." Alyce lifts her weary eyes to his, voice soft. "There is nowhere else."

Percy leads Alyce up the stairs, her form swaying under his touch. He swings open the spare room, gentle morning light filters through the open window, winds shifting the gossamer curtains.

"I hope this is enough space for you, I'll grab you another blanket if needed."

"It's perfect." Alyce turns to him, carefully, as if she might fall. Percy reluctantly pulls his arm from her.

"You'd better rest." He leans against the open doorframe after she sits on the bed. "There is a bathroom and *amazing* shower through that door. I'll find some herbs for fevers, be back in a bit."

"Promise?" Her voice stops him. His eyes find her face, so delicate and small. His palms could cup her ash dark cheeks. His thumbs could lightly rest on her lips, pinkies wrapping the back of her ears.

He told her once he would return. That was two days ago. Making promises and already breaking them. He levels his eyes to hers, grey as the ink filled moon and underbelly of birds.

A grin touches the corner of his mouth. "Yes. Promise."

Alyce sighs visibly, her worn coat and hospital gown filthy. Hair spiked every direction.

Percy wants to stay, ask her why she needed to flee, why she never arrived at the station and why his heart beats so much near her. He doesn't, though. He closes her door with a click and heads down the stairs, rummaging through the cupboards.

"What are you doing?" Sol snips, making Percy jump.

"Getting herbs, for Alyce."

"Ah, go out to the gardens." Sol grumbles.

"Right." Percy slaps his forehead. "Fresh is always better than dried." He moves to the door, then stops, turning back to Sol.

"Did you... recognize Alyce?" Asks Percy.
Sol shrugs. "I'm not so good with faces anymore."

But Percy knows that is a lie. Sol hasn't forgotten a face in forty years.

Percy knocks on Alyce's door half an hour later, a steaming cup of herbal tea in his hands. No response. Percy creaks open the door, eyeing a slim figure under the covers.

Alyce is asleep. Her hair a damp halo around her, the smell of flower shampoo rising from the bed.

Percy sets the cup on the nightstand with a small *tink*. She doesn't move.

Percy sighs, running a hand through his hair. He doesn't mean to stay, but somehow finds himself thumbing through his loaned poetry book, enjoying the fact she wrote next to his words. Letters are stuffed between the pages, and his story takes up most of the back. He flips to the beginning of the book, reading her bold script, as if this were a title to a story they both were writing.

I Am The Sun

Alyce turns, groaning in her rest. Percy hesitates, then presses a hand to her forehead. Heat blooms under his touch. She's burning up.

"Alyce. Alyce." He taps her cheek, she moans but doesn't wake.

"Sol!" Percy hollers down the hall. "I need cold rags and more willow bark."

"On it." Sol shuffles in the floor below.

"Hold on, Alyce." He presses his hand to her cheek.

"She shouldn't be this ill. I know she was treated at the hospital; traveling might have worn her down, same with running from…whatever it was she ran from. I- I don't know what to do and I'm a nurse!" Percy paces, hands on his head, the curls straightened and poofy through his running fingers.

"The first thing to do is *calm down*. The girl is going to be fine."

"You don't know that." Percy practically growls.

"I do, in fact."

The floors creak under his rhythmic footsteps.

"Percy, listen to me. Go to Sara. Tell her I need a bottle of Alom Afiya; I don't have time to make one and she'll have some on hand."

"Alom Afi-" Percy freezes. This only confirmed his thoughts. He saw the discarded tangled roots on her bedside table. He knew what that meant. Still, he cannot help the words pouring from his mouth. "You mean she's-"

"I'm not saying anything, to you." He adds. "She didn't eat this morning and was wary of the windows."

"Alom need light too-"

"Not all. Some need darkness, others need a different kind of light. I am unsure which is needed in this case, but Sara will give you a general mixture. Anything will be better. Go!" His snap sends Percy dashing. Throwing on a coat and diving toward the door.

"But if she worsens-"

"She'll worsen more if she doesn't get that Afiya. Earth knows what she was given at Halo."

Percy wracks his brain, trying to remember if he ever saw her consume light. Never. Even the sunlamps were kept off. His steps hasten.

"Hopefully I'll be back before nightfall."

"Only if you run, boy."

Percy gives him a hard stare. "That is just what I intend to do."

Sol chuckles.

Darkness wraps the forest in tendril hands. Fog shifts over the ground and through the trees a living thing. Percy runs. He has never run so hard or fast in his life. His feet pound the forest floor, he leaps fallen trees and lifted roots and old stones which have lost their voice.

His breath is a fire in his lungs, body screaming for rest. Night rises as the ocean tide and still he does not stop.

The healer lives in the center of the woods, deep between hidden glens and the seashore.

Percy only slows when smoke fills his nose, threatening to choak him in hurt filled memories.

He crashes to the ground before the healer's hut, breath escaping him as his lungs reach for it. A light spills over his face but he doesn't move. A woman materializes before him, as if birthed of light. Green hair straight as a new willow bough, twisting boughs rise through tangled strands, branches sticking out in every direction, showing her age.

She will be Tree soon. Her body aching for roots, blood to sap and breath to leaves. She will return to the form of their forefathers, the Trees of Arian. Bark covers her face, obscuring features, her hands and bare arms.

She extends a knobbed hand to him, pulling Percy to his feet. She searches his face for a moment, seeing *through* him. Seeing all of him.

"Come in. I know why you are here."

Percy ducks, entering her small home. A bed sits in the corner, shelves of tonics and herbs and bottles of Afiya line the walls, casting a soft rainbow of colorful glows. A cluttered worktable takes up most of the space and Sara dances around to the other side. Her slim, knotted hands reaching for herbs and bottles of light.

"Your friend is ill, yeah?"

"Yes. Running a fever and weak. She hasn't absorbed any Afiya, mixed for Etz's, that is. Sol said you would have something for individuals in need of other types of light." Percy wipes his palms on his pants, nervous from her sudden glare.

"Do not mistake me as someone petty from war. The ill are the ill, no divisions. Tell me her needs."

Percy doesn't ask how she knows about Alyce, he doesn't want to waste the time. "Something for her weakness, something for her heart, something for her mind. She is ill and sad and afraid, and I will do anything you ask if you will help her."

That stills the healer's busy hands, her bark face and dark eyes find his. "And for you?" She pauses, then continues to work in haste.

"What of your weakness, your heart, your mind? You are struggling also." She casts him a dark glance. "Bring me that Afiya there, the one to your right."

Percy is gentle lifting the bottle free, passing it over the table. It hums in his hands, whispered words in the soft silver glow.

"Your friend needs moonlight, dark stars and distant luminance. She is Alom, I can feel it."

"Sol is Alom, he drinks sun Afiya."

"Sol is labradorite, he needs the strength of the sun. Your friend is different."

"What is she?"

Sara closes her eyes. "I sense changes needed, one way of being drifting into another... interesting."

"But this will work for her?" Percy points to the new bottle being mixed in swirls of silvers and inky blacks.

Sara nods. "This should suffice until Sol can make moon Afiya. He knows how. It's a long process, one month of work for a single bottle. Prominent though, it will last her a while; she may need more in the beginning if she is this ill." The cap placed, Sara sets the tonic aside.

"And for you?"

"What about me?"

Sara's gaze arches. "You need hope, dear Percy Waiden. You need passion again."

"Survival is a passion." He jokes.

"Survival is not meaningless, yes, but we are not machines, we do not run on programing and codes. You need sunlight, air, water, breath. You need joy and hope and rest. You need tears to carry away your hurt and peace to grow a new garden in your soul. You need excitement for life, Percy." She rounds the table, places a hand on his cheek. "And don't tell me you are undeserving- your pride is not that great."

Pride. His guilt over living- tied to pride? He almost laughs, but needs to bite the inside of his cheeks and blink stinging tears.

"I'm trying." He gets out, all his hurt breaking over him in waves. He pulls away. "I have to go now, I need to get back before dawn."

"Take this." Sara presses a folded parchment in his hands. "Open when you are ready, and not before." She winks, giving him a smile.

Percy ducks out the door, Sara standing in the light of her home.

"May Earth speed your footsteps."

"Thanks." He gives her a smile, small and genuine. Then he disappears back into the woods, wishing he could move through the darkness like water and wind. Instead he runs, heavy and loud and lungs throbbing.

But he doesn't stop. Not once.

Alyce is dreaming. She lays in the gray dust of the moon. Whole and happy.

She is Nadala, penning letters to her golden haired love and sending them along the heavenly ocean to be held and treasured in his hands. She cherishes his letters in return.

She is Nadala, and she runs along her handmade bridge, unable to contain her joy.

She is Nadala, and she is falling, crashing into the sea with all the force of a hurricane.

She is Nadala, rising out of empty despair to meet her love…

"Are you awake?" The voice only faintly familiar, a hand cool on her brow.

Alyce groans, shaking herself awake. Her eyelids heavy, the room spinning.

"Here, drink this." A vial pressed to her lips. A mindless swallow. Light floods her arteries. Alyce's eyes shoot open and she rolls onto her side, stomach heaving out of fear.

"It's moon Afiya." The man says quickly, holding out waiting hands if she rolls from the bed. Alyce gasps, leaning back.

"It's good." She closes her eyes. "Can I have some more?"

The man, Sol, she remembers now, passes her the bottle. Alyce drinks more than half of it, her body starved.

"Thank the Divine Hum." She murmurs. Sol chuckles. She studies him from the corner of her eye.

"You worked for my father."

Sol presses a finger to his lips, eyes drawing her gaze to the corner of the room. Percy asleep, curled under a blanket, dwarfing the chair he rests in.

"He ran all night to get you this." Sol taps her bottle. Alyce clutches it tight.

"Why?"

Sol almost laughs. "The boy cares for you. And he's a nurse. He should be a healer, with the head he's got on his shoulders, and the heart in his chest."

Sol tears his eyes from Percy, studying her again. "I did know your father. I worked for the Radian Guard. I was a General." His chest puffs a little. "Percy saved my life. In the battle." He doesn't elaborate. Alyce doesn't question the fact Percy would do something like that, save an enemy commander, because she knows him, too.

"I wrote to him after the war and a terrible loss." Sol shakes his head. "Waiden traveled four hundred miles to start over."

"What made him move in with… you?" She doesn't finish her sentence and she doesn't need to.

"To live with an enemy General? I liked the boy, saw him face the worst moment of his life with more kindness than anyone I'd met. I knew, despite the battle lines between us, I wanted to know more about him. Help him if I could, but also learn. I had been kind, once; I wanted to be kind again."

"We often bury our kindness in times of trouble. Claiming we must protect ourselves. In reality, I think we only lose the most vital part of us."

Sol nods at her words, leaning back in his chair.

"Will you tell my father I am here? You must know he is looking for me."

"I don't keep up to date with Radius gossip." Sol waves a grey green hand. "I am an Alom who loves the sun, hence my move to Ulna. No, dear, I will not be telling anyone you are here. Unless you would like me to?"

Alyce shakes her head.

Sol groans as he stands, hands on his knees for support. "You are welcome to stay as long as you need, with the fee of helping around the inn. I've been trying to fix this place up for years now. Once you are well again, of course."

Alyce thanks him softly, Sol closing the door with a light click.

She clutches her moon Afiya, digging out the bottle Percy gave her. One for sun, one for moon. How perfect. She watches Percy rest for a time, his chest rising and falling like the tide. Perhaps he is the ocean, and she the observing star, distant and bright. How beautiful he is, she thinks to herself. The afternoon glow hitting his cheeks and illuminating his golden hair and curled boughs. A green leaf has sprouted from one bough, no bigger than her pinky.

She longs for his eyes to open so she might count the shades of brown his irises contain, but not yet. Let him sleep a while longer, dreaming and easy. She will wait. She will always wait for him.

Percy stumbles down the stairs a while later, night having fallen outside once more.

Alyce jumps when he leans against the kitchen frame, his eyes wide. "You're awake."

"So are you." She laughs.

Percy's smile grows. He crosses the room and Alyce wants him to stop in front of her. To speak something wonderful as he always does. But Percy slumps in a chair, head in his hands and dark moons under his eyes.

"I was so worried, Alyce. I mean," he laughs, leaning back. "I'm a nurse, and a soldier. We're taught to keep our cool-"

"Yeah, no cool was kept." Sol chimes in, mixing a large bowl of Afiya. Herbs and ions and song.

"Shut up." Percy groans, laying his head on the table. "Why didn't you tell me?"
Suddenly those brown eyes are stuck on hers. Deep and dark as oceans and mountain roots.

Alyce looks down, circling the rim of her cup with a dark hued finger. "I needed to protect myself-"

"In doing so you only caused yourself more harm-"

"Boy, let her finish." Sol pipes in, setting a warm cup of Afiya before Percy.

Percy runs a shaking hand through his hair, spiking guilt through Alyce's chest.

"I didn't want anyone to know I was Alom, peace treaty or no. There was no one I trusted." She meets his eyes. "Even my own people."

Percy's eyes widen, shock, or maybe understanding in them.

Alyce sips, breaking the visual contact.

"It doesn't matter why you are here, Alyce." Percy stands with a sigh. "Sol knows how to make the Afiya you need, you'll never need to deprive yourself again." He gives a tight smile, rising from his seat, eyes cast from her to Sol. "I'm going back to sleep."

Alyce waits until Percy has stumbled back up the stairs, downing the rest of her Afiya. "Is he angry with me?"

Sol shakes his head. "No. He doesn't have the fire for it. Percy is a man who takes on too many troubles, thinking he can hold the pain so others don't have to." Sol chuckles. "That rarely works, but he tries."

"I'm strong enough to bear my own pain." Alyce curls her fist under the table.

"Oh, I'm sure you are, knowing your father. He wanted you to join the Guard, yes?"

Alyce nods.

"That's not the point. Percy will take the war, the starvation, the prejudice, the loss of *everyone*, into himself, thinking he can heal it- restore what was lost."

Alyce frowns. "Percy believes we should seek healing ourselves. Reach for our own light rather than be reliant on someone else."

Sol gestures in agreement. "As we should. But he must remind himself of that also. We forget," Sol smiles softly. "The garden was made for rest."

CHANGING

TIDES

xii.

The paper slips under Alyce's door with a sigh. The sound right and good in her soul. She slips off the bed, scooping it up with careful hands. The shuffle of feet fade before she opens the parchment, the scent of fresh ink blooming into her moonlit room.

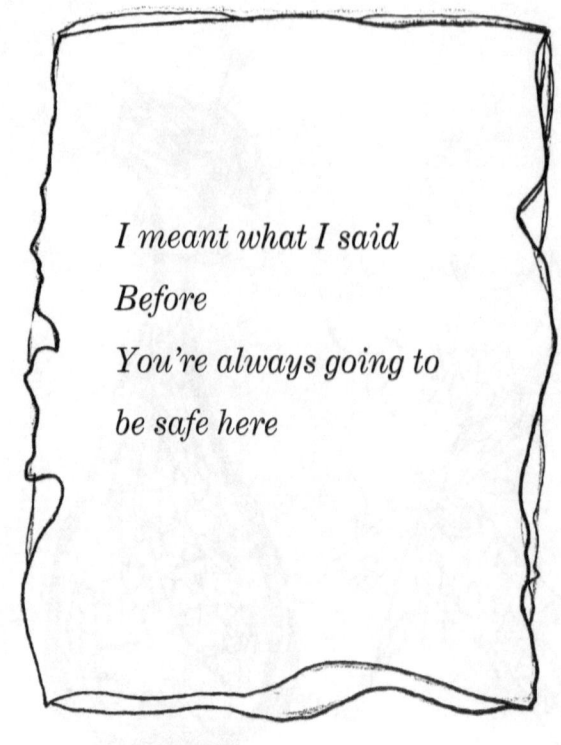

I meant what I said

Before

You're always going to

be safe here

She presses the letter to her chest, cherishing his words.

It's a mad dash around the room, digging through desk drawers and searching through repurposed mugs for pens. Finding only dusty charcoal and faded pieces of newspaper, she writes.

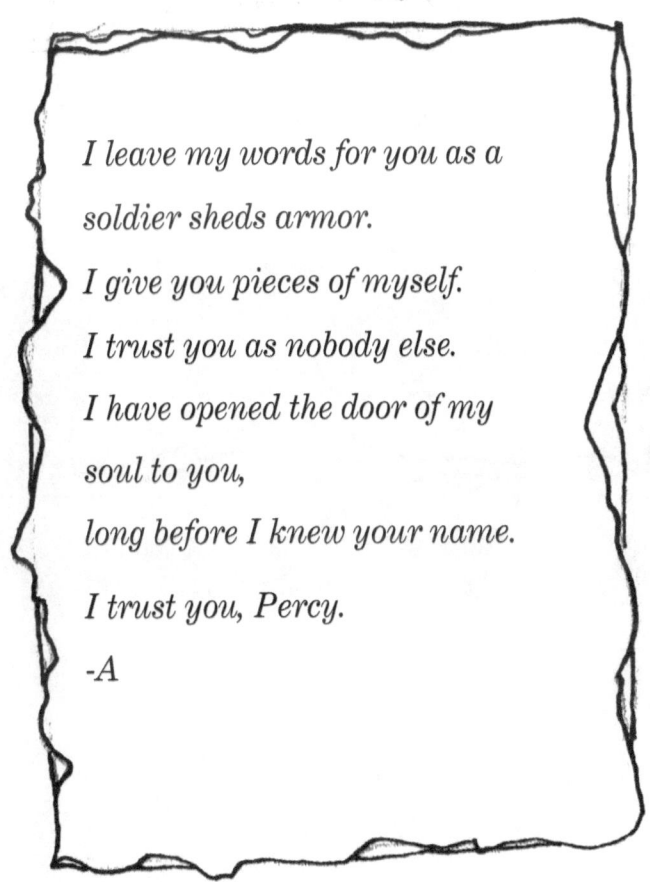

I leave my words for you as a

soldier sheds armor.

I give you pieces of myself.

I trust you as nobody else.

I have opened the door of my

soul to you,

long before I knew your name.

I trust you, Percy.

-A

*I know what it means to release
armor.
Unbind the stitching of long
kept hardships and lost faith.
It is like digging stones from
your soul, baring your gaping
self to others.*

*I know what it is to fear.
I know what it is to lose.*

I don't want to lose you,

Alyce.

P.

Never.

-A

Alyce wakes with the dawn, before dawn really. Her face lifted to the last moonlight, she slips into the gardens, mouthing soft words to the moon. She enjoys the first aurora of dawn. Sometimes Percy joins her, but rarely. Most mornings she finds him asleep in his bed when she walks past his door, biting the inside of her cheeks to keep in her grin.

Sol greets her when she comes into the kitchen, and they get to work.

"Afiya is precarious to make, takes time and diligence. The Ion Trees have not been bearing as much fruit, so we must draw on other elements for our light." Sol taps sticky light off his wooden spoon. "This batch will be left in the windows. A weeks' time, we'll have golden Afiya. Here, try." Sol holds a tasting pick out to her.

Alyce has only a lick, the sunlight strong through her veins. "Could use honey."
Sol chuckles.

"What are we making?" Percy yawns, slipping into the kitchen. Baggy shirt and long pants baring the scent of sleep.

"It's almost noon." Alyce points out, the sun dial visible through the curved kitchen windows.

"Ah, let him sleep. Got a lot to regulate in yourself, eh, boy?"

"I guess?" Percy musses with his hair. Alyce's fingers twitch.

"I'll try to get back on a schedule, it's hard now that I'm not working full time- sleep is so irresistible. What's this?" He tries to poke at the bowl.

Percy jumps back at Sol's sudden grin. "Renovating time." Sol cackles, rubbing his hands together. "Follow this recipe, call if you need help." Sol passes her a worn paper.

Alyce skims the words-

4 cups of love, taken from tree's exhale.

5 tsp of rainwater, caught in a silver cup.

1 crushed crystal, rolled in a copper bowl.

Mix well and add ions. Will be sticky at first.

Fruit or flowers as desired. Note: Place moon

Afiya in open area each sunset and

gather before sunrise.

Alyce shakes out the paper, tiny purple flowers falling from the creases.

She sets to work.

The boys set to a day of heat and retiling the roof, which needs more repair than Percy let on. Alyce finishes the Afiya batch and starts on another. This one she sprinkles lavender petals and leafy stems

through soft purple light and will leave outside at
dusk. This one will wait a whole month before it's
ready to ingest, needing a full moon cycle of light
infused into the water and ions.

"Lunch!" Alyce brings lemon Afiya out to the
boys, waiting in the shade under a twisting pine, as
if hiding from the sun.

"Thank the Divine." Percy swipes his brow,
leaving a streak of dirt.

"How is the Afiya?" Sol sips from his cup.

"I brought samples of my first batch. Here." She
passes them each a small cup. Sol sniffs his,
swirling the navy and violet liquid. "Interesting
color."

"It should be done, this one is midday sunlight.
Energizing and invigorating."

Percy gives her a trusting smile, downing his.

His eye twitches, lips pull slowly into a grimace as
he swallows.

Sol takes a careful sip. Then gags, doubling over.

"Are you alright?" Alyce drops her tray, but Percy
is there first, pounding the older man on the
backside.

"Swallow it." He orders. "She's your pupil."

Sol swallows, coming up for air.

"Elderberry?" He guesses. Alyce lifts her tray from the grass.

"Yes."

"The elder needs at *least* five hours of sun light, to nullify the acidity. And some sweetener." He drinks the last of his cup, smacking his lips like an expert. "Good foundation, though. Shows potential."

"That's great," Percy gasps out, giving Alyce a shaky thumbs up. "You'll do good."

"Percy, your face is green." Alyce extends worried hands to him.

"He'll be fine, won't you boy?" Sol smacks Percy on the back, returning the favor.
Percy yelps and Sol grins.

"Let's cheat and put a bit of stevia in this one. Come on, I'll show you how." Sol guides them inside and Alyce bites the insides of her cheeks.

Percy mulls over papers at the kitchen table, scribbling furiously, inking and stamping envelopes.

Sol guides Alyce through another batch, this one roses and evening light.
It is the color of winter sunsets and warm, crimson light, swirling with pinks and yellows and golds. Alyce takes only the smallest bite, less than half her pinky nail, the light sending shivers through her bones.

Someday, she thinks, I will be able to stand under the full sun and not be afraid of breaking.

Percy hands her another folded letter, and Alyce stuffs it into a cream envelope.

A growing stack sits before them on the table, titles of curling ink in the midday heat.

The market bustles around them, bottles of colored Afiya stacked on their table, a basket with sealed letters. Others hawk their wares and wave ribboned fingers at customers. Rows of stalls line the grove of trees, shaded and bright and color filled. People walk from stall to stall, eyeing wares. Children dash with silky ribbons on their wrists, as if their arms are wings and they run to take flight.

Baskets of ion are gathered and sold. High prices showing their rarity. Showing the desperation the Stonefloor has caused.

"I didn't know you did this." Alyce sits under a large umbrella Percy bought, a rimmed hat covering her head and almost all of her body covered under Percy's inside-out military coat and a baggy, floral patterned dress, belted at her waist.

Percy chuckles, sealing another letter. "There's a lot you don't know about me."

Alyce rolls her eyes, smirking. "Should I be worried?"

"No." His voice serious now. "When Sol started doing the markets, I saw this as an opportunity to..."

"Spread hope?" Alyce offers.

"Encourage people. We all need a love letter now and then." Percy scratches his neck, thin green scars on his hand shining in the light. "So, I started writing and leaving them in this basket, open for anyone to take."

Alyce skims through the pile. Titles of *For Grief, For Anger, For Loss, For Joy, For Peace, For a Good Nights Sleep, For Stillness,* peek at her from Percy's flowing script.

"It's a beautiful mission."

"Yeah." Percy agrees, still smiling, hand still on his neck, thumb tracing his right clavicle. Alyce places her hand over his.

He stills. Deathly calm, his eyes watch her. He doesn't move.

Alyce takes his hand in hers, thumb tracing the pale scars on his fingers and palm. Her hand finds his neck, breath fingers width apart. A long scar juts down from the back of his neck to his collar bone, where Alyce traces the ridge of a once broken bone, now bumpy with mis-repair.

Percy's hand covers hers. Alyce can see the shards of metal slicing Percy's skin. Knows the impact of a body thrown from explosion. Feel the pain of loss. The pain of being broken and torn. His memories burn inside him, Alyce can almost reach them- So many scars! Her Alom mind able to access them. To see as he saw and feel as he felt.

A thumb runs over her cheek, damp with tears. Her tears.

"Sorry." She smiles, pulling away, wiping her cheeks.

"Alyce," Percy tugs on her hand, she turns back to him. "Let me share my memories by my choice."

"O-of course! I'm sorry, Percy-"

He shakes his head, smiling. "It's alright. Hey, it is alright." Both his hands are cupping her cheeks now, his hands hot against her skin.

Percy ducks his head a little, meeting her watery gaze. His eyes are sunlight, warm and powerful.

Alyce pulls away, cheeks cool without his touch, pushing back her coat and lifting the dress up over her hip. Percy's cheeks burn and he checks no one is watching them under their canopy.

"Here." Alyce taps her hip, a wicked scar, raised and angry, cuts above her iliac crest.

Percy sucks in a breath and Alyce drops her dress. "You know about the others. This is one most people don't find."

A woman bustles over, interrupting them, lifting a bottle of emerald Afiya from the shelf. Percy finishes the transaction, a smile coming over his face as he tells her, "It's good for quiet afternoon naps."

The woman sighs, running a hand over her brow. "That is what I need."

"Please, take this, too." Alyce holds up a letter. She takes both, paying for the Afiya with a half coin, Percy giving her the discount price.

The woman leaves and Percy's smile falls.

"Alyce." He turns to her. She takes a half step back.

"What happened?" His voice is so gentle, she almost doesn't fall into the memory of her father, training her with swords instead of wooden blades, claiming she was a Yahalom. But Alyce's skin is not the hard stone of the clan she was born to, her flesh is soft as bark and the blade cut through her instead of shattering.

"It was an accident. I got sick afterward. I don't remember much."

"Come here." Percy flexes his palm, fist to open, open to fist.

She doesn't hesitate, not even when his hand lands lightly over her hip, fingers gentle on the scar palpable even through the clothing. The contact is

124

only a second, then his hand rests on her chest, over her lungs.

"May the Divine Hum be your Healer. May you be open to healing."

Alyce places a hand over his jagged clavicle, murmuring the repeated words. Her hand longs to trace the path of his bones. To learn the circular flow of his chlorophyll blood. She takes a half step closer.

"Do you have any apple?" A small voice breaks them apart.

Percy grins, genuine and bright. "I sure do." He pulls a bottle from behind the counter, kept safe. "And give this to your mom." He passes along a letter with the Afiya.

The boy, no older than ten, eyes Alyce suspiciously with coco orbs.

"Do I know you?"

Alyce leans against the table, shrugging. "I don't know, do you?"

The boy hums, hand on his chin. "You read to my mommy?"

It's a question.

"Room four, garden magazines."

"Yes!" Little Chalo jumps up and down, clapping his hands.

"I remember." Alyce snaps, grinning. "How is your mom?"

"She's good." He picks at their tablecloth. "I have to go now, dad is waiting."

"Tell your mom I said hi." Alyce waves.

"Me too!" Percy chimes in. "Silver Afiya and sage will help with eyesight. I already put some in your Afiya order."

"Thanks." Chalo skips away, disappearing into the crowd.

"You should be a healer, Percy."

"I am? Thanks?"

"No." Alyce laughs. "Custom batches of Afiya. Handwritten prayers. Genuine friendship. That's more important than nurses prescribing drugs and cold hospitals."

"Hospitals are necessary. Surgery and meds and intensive care has saved lives."

"I know, it's saved mine. I just mean...the healing that comes after. Repairing the soul is important. Maybe more so."

Percy shuffles through Afiya bottles and stacks loose letters. "Sol makes most of our Afiya, but custom batches would need more time. I already write letters and send prayers to all my patients. Or I used to. I'd need a space to work and see people from, even beds for the severely ill. At that point I'd need staff. There's laundry, herbs, paperwork, billing-"

"It seems like you've thought about this."

"I have."

"Enough to talk yourself out of it?" Alyce tugs the letter from his hands, meeting earth brown eyes. By the Divine, she loves the earth.

Percy looks away. He peeks up from their umbrella. "The sun will be setting soon. We should pack while we have the shade."

xiii.

Percy guides them up the shaded hill toward the inn, laden with their folded table, the umbrella hanging over his shoulder, the Afiya shelf causing his arm to quiver. They needed something lighter weight.

Alyce is quiet beside him, carrying the basket of letters and carefully packed box of Afiya bottles, the tablecloth resting on top.

"Are you alright?" Alyce glances up at him, light hitting the Afiya, casting a rainbow upon her skin.

"All good." Percy huffs.

"Wait." Alyce stops behind him, Percy laboriously turns, catching her in a slant of sunlight before she steps back into the lengthening shadows.

"The orchard."

Percy follows her gaze, the straight tree lines beyond the short stone wall.

"They're dying."

The trees are black with rot, ion fruit in heaps at their decaying trunks.

"It's the Stonefloor. Old remains of the war."
Percy explains, dropping his load, stretching his
neck. "The roots cannot harvest ions from the
earth, so they die."

Alyce sets down her load, eyes saddened. "The
sheets of stone underground will destroy Ulna's
roots. If it doesn't stop, everything will die. My
people did this."

Before he can blink, Alyce is up and over the
wall, skirts caught in the wind, a flash of muted
colors. "Where are you going?" Percy chases after
her.

Alyce doesn't stop. The stench does not deter her,
nor the unstable and sinking ground, pitfalls
waiting to catch them. This is a battlefield itself, a
graveyard of last breaths.

Alyce stops before Percy has run out of air,
gripping the hem of her dress. (They needed to go
shopping.)

Percy can hear the ache in the trees, their pain.
He squeezes his eyes closed.

"Look." Alyce grips his hand, pointing.

There, bathed in fading sunlight, is an ion tree.
Its fruit ripe and humming and ocher. It stands,
not the tallest, but the strongest, persevering on.
Pushing through the cracks of the stone and
finding life. One tree, amid thousands in decay.

"Here." Alyce reaches for a fruit.

"Let me." Percy steps forward, reaching a firm orb above their heads. The fruit pulses with light, dark skin containing galaxies of tiny stars. "Don't want to be repeating history."

Alyce crosses her arms. "Very funny. Maybe you should be saving me, not joining me in damnation."

"Maybe I couldn't bear to lose you." Percy takes the first bite, earth hued gaze locked on hers.

She flushes and triumph soars through him.

Determining it safe, he passes her the rest. Juices drip down their chins and starhoney blooms on their tongues. Alyce grins at him, childish. "I've never had an ion fruit."

"Well, you'll never forget your first." Percy laughs, wiping juice from her chin with his thumb.

Her frequency. So different from any Alom he's known, any Etz for that matter. She is like the earth. Healing, rich and vibrant. Calm. Energetic and kind and funny. Percy cannot remember the last time he smiled so much. Really smiled.

He is in love with the earth.

Finished fruit still damp on their mouths, Alyce bends to the earth. Presses a hand into the loam and lichen and rot.

"Divine, heal this land." Percy whispers, putting two fingers to his lips, touching it to the bark of this perfect tree.

The door swings open after sunset. Percy dropping the shelf and table with a sigh. He takes the Afiya from Alyce next, settling the clinking bottles aside on a designated shelf. Alyce straitens their market things, the table, umbrella and shelf resting in a cove behind the stairs.

Alyce pulls off her boots and tugs the war jacket from her shoulders. She leaves both in the foyer.

Percy shuffles through things for tomorrow, payment chips, clean boots, a nicer jacket than he usually bothers with.

Alyce gives him a tired smile, the stairs creaking under her steps. Percy watches her disappear into the darkness of the upper floor. He continues to stare after she has closed her door, hearing her footsteps above.

He runs a hand through his hair, mussing golden curls. His heart pounds inside his chest, filling and emptying his lungs too quick.

"You alright, boy?" Sol pads from the kitchen, fingers stained violet.

"I don't know, Sol. I honestly do not."

Percy towels his hair, drying his boughs with a quick rub. There are new sprouts along his boughs,

tiny green shoots growing pointed leaves. New
growth along his arteries and veins and life lines.
Roots seeking ground.

His hands are trembling and he rubs his face,
massaging along his scalp.
His spider plant shimmies on his desk, concerned
leaves reaching out for him.
Percy kisses soft fingers to the green leaves, a
couple tendrils encircling his hand, giving him a
leafy embrace.

A soft *shhhh*, a sigh upon his floor. Paper sliding
across wooden floors.

The letter beckons him like moonlight, moon eyes
and soft touches, glowing upon his floor in bleeding
white. He untangles himself from the spider plant,
reaching for the waiting words.

Percy sits against his bed on the floor, opening
slowly her unveiled thoughts.

I shouldn't have pried;

I have no right.

Memories are fickle things and I have no choice which ones present themselves when I choose to look for them, but often I find they are ones of great emotion.

Bubbling joy. Anger. Soft happiness. Pride.
Condemnation.
Pain.

I know what it is to bear pain alone.
To be buried in guilt.

For your own sake, do not be buried alone when

I am right next door.

-A

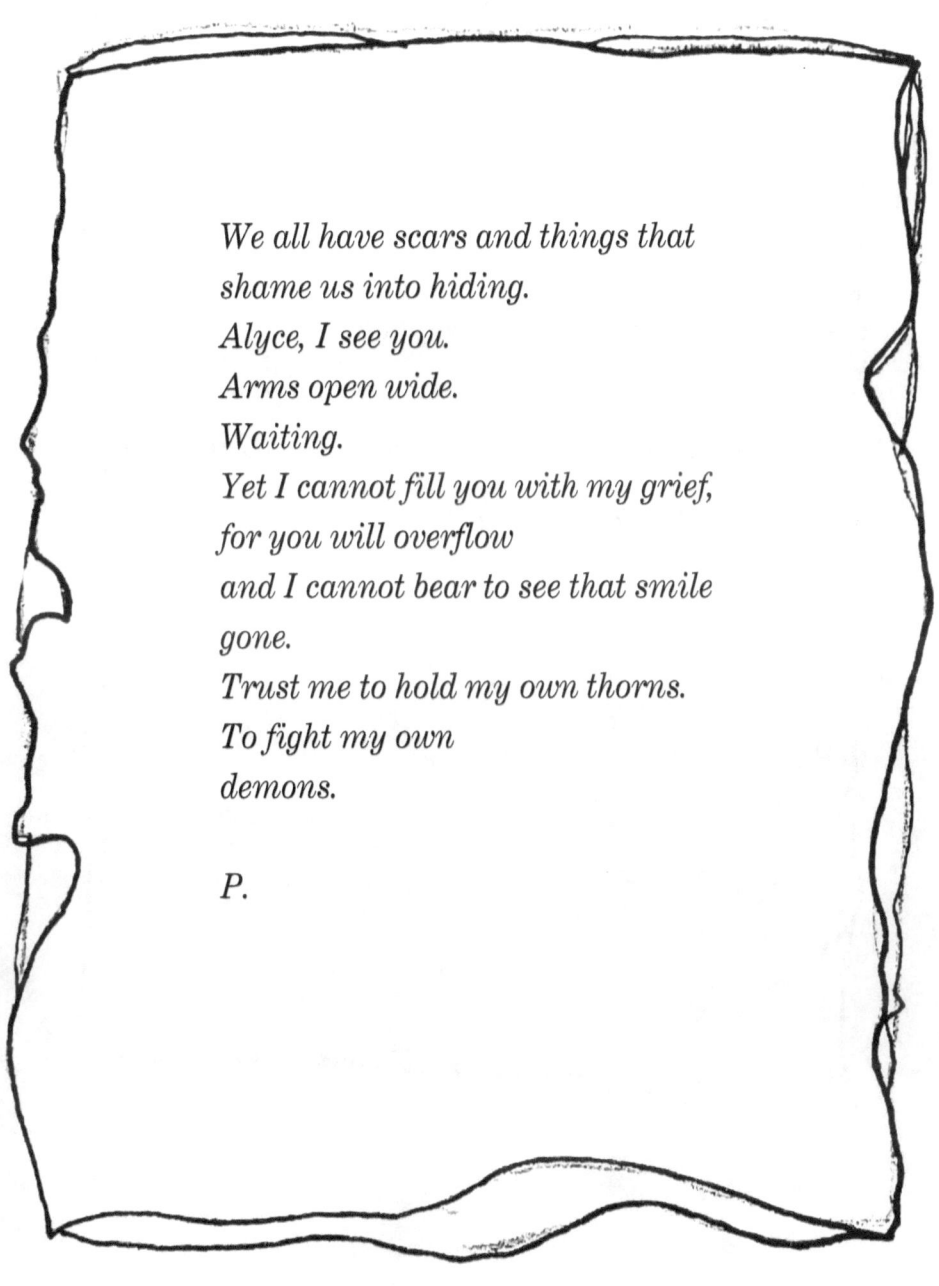

We all have scars and things that
shame us into hiding.
Alyce, I see you.
Arms open wide.
Waiting.
Yet I cannot fill you with my grief,
for you will overflow
and I cannot bear to see that smile
gone.
Trust me to hold my own thorns.
To fight my own
demons.

P.

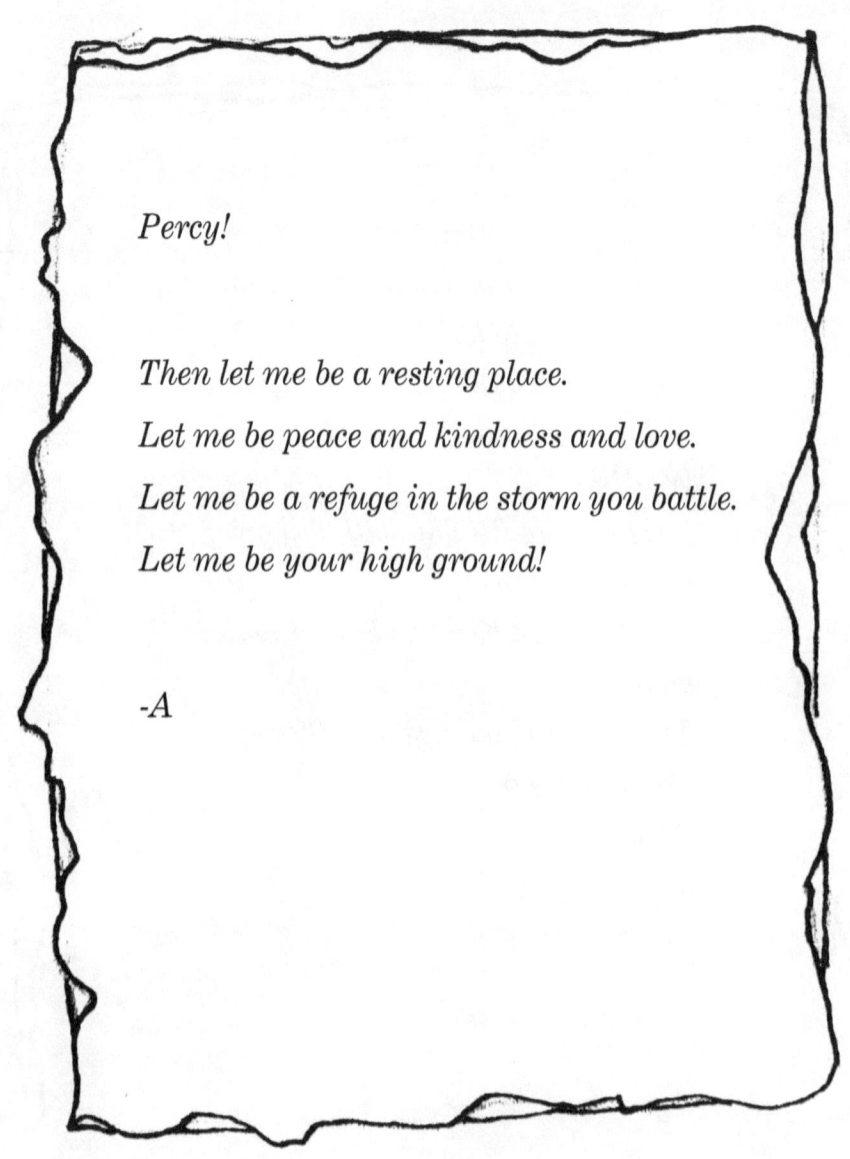

Percy!

Then let me be a resting place.
Let me be peace and kindness and love.
Let me be a refuge in the storm you battle.
Let me be your high ground!

-A

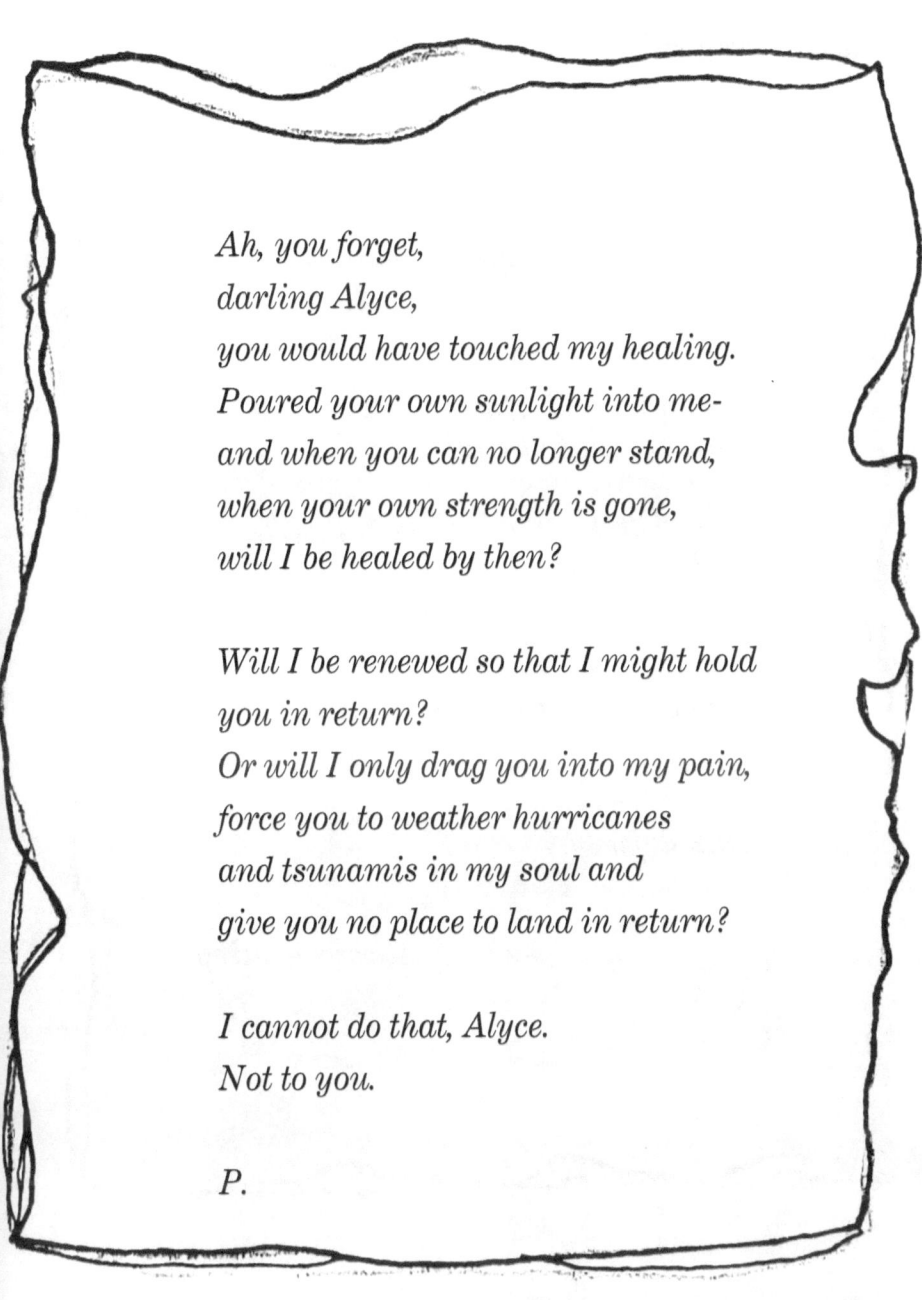

Ah, you forget,
darling Alyce,
you would have touched my healing.
Poured your own sunlight into me—
and when you can no longer stand,
when your own strength is gone,
will I be healed by then?

Will I be renewed so that I might hold
you in return?
Or will I only drag you into my pain,
force you to weather hurricanes
and tsunamis in my soul and
give you no place to land in return?

I cannot do that, Alyce.
Not to you.

P.

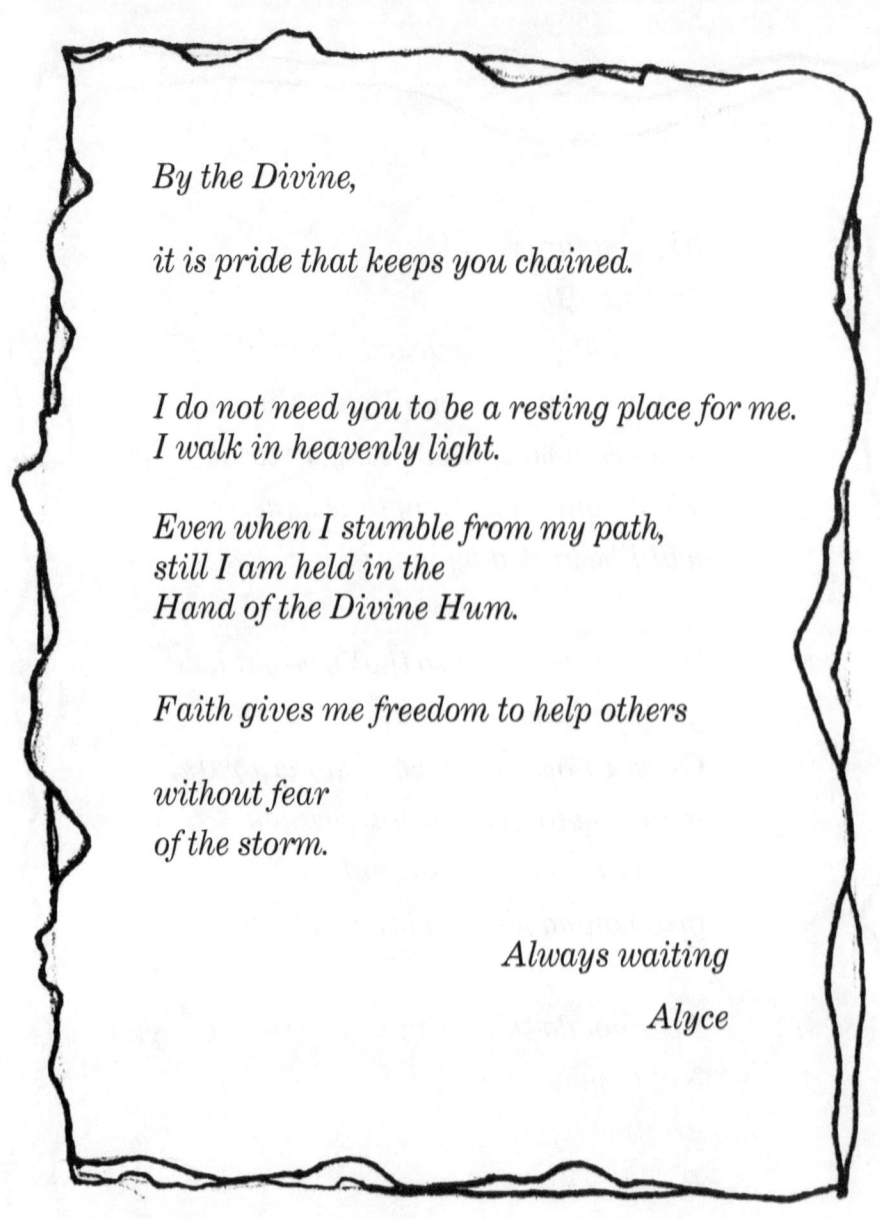

By the Divine,

it is pride that keeps you chained.

I do not need you to be a resting place for me.
I walk in heavenly light.

Even when I stumble from my path,
still I am held in the
Hand of the Divine Hum.

Faith gives me freedom to help others

without fear
of the storm.

Always waiting

Alyce

Tears dot her crumpled page.
Percy pulls her words closer, holding them tight.
He doesn't let go.

Percy doesn't move from his spot on the floor, fearing the dislodgement of this…anguish, which has kept him from shore. Kept him in an ocean he cannot navigate and grows tired of treading to stay alive.

Bowing his head, he holds out his hands.

"I do not know how to walk in the light. I do not know how to rest in the dark. I do not know how to face what I am."

His hands tremble, breath soft.

"You know the things I have done."

There is a light before him, a divine presence. Placing a hand on his damp cheek, wiping away glimmering tears.

"I am here." The Light says, a hand on his chest. *"I have always been with you. Do not think I have not seen the work of your hands. Wicked and wonderful alike. I have given my all so you might be free."*

"What would you have me do? To be free?" He's sobbing now, the tears a release. A pain and sharp ache, an inhale of new breath. "I don't want to be sad anymore. I don't want to find my mind wandering to lost days and faces I cannot remember.

I want to be free from this guilt weighing me down. It was my-y fault. Ev- everything was my fault."

"What is fault but a lesson learned? You cannot know the path of your actions. You can only choose the next step."

Suddenly it is Ojo kneeling before him, hands cupping his cheeks. His heart. The voice of the Divine flowing through him.

"Breathe, big brother. Just breathe."

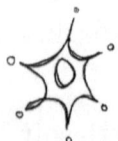

A quiet tap, the lightest rap of his knuckles. The door opens as if she was waiting for him, hand already on the knob, muscles and tendons ready to engage.

"Alyce-"

It's the only word he can form before she's looping her arms around his torso, face buried in his chest. She's trembling. His heart quickens, strong and fast.

Her eyes match his only because they are ringed crystal with unshed tears.

Percy's arms wrap around her, hands pulling her closer. There is no space between them. No room for words.

Only this moment; a shared breath.

"I apologize, Alyce." Percy says into her short, tight coils. "You were right, I have too much pride in myself."

"There is so much goodness in you, Percy." Her hands clutch his shirt, fists white. She finds his eyes with fierce silver orbs.

"I know." One hand cups her cheek, thumb tracing her zygomatic bone.

She realises her hold, a dark palm finds his heart. She leans into him, her weight perfect. She's fragile, a gentle winged creature, fluttering in his palm.

"Alyce, you're crying."

She stiffens, as if realizing a mistake. His gaze slipping past a barrier she hadn't intended him to see.

Too swift, she steps away, the space of the hall between them, her room an anchor, fist planted on the frame.

Her eyes are on his, warring between logic and emotion. Percy fears his heart might explode. Perhaps this is the moment that breaks them. The one where everything changes.

But Alyce steps away, sliding her door shut, and Percy bites the inside of his cheeks.

A beat. Two. Theirs. Hearts full of panic and want.

"I love you, Percy." Her voice muffled through the door, needing protection to bare these words. Percy leans against the wood, pulled in by her force.

"You barely know me." He teases, yet heat blooms in his chest.

"I don't need to know you to love you. Just knowing you are in pain or ever have been makes me ache inside. I feel your hurt, too. I *know*."

He stills, listening, head against the wood. Inches dividing them by miles.

"Just let me be close to you, if only to sit beside you and watch your thunder roll. I would wait out your storm with you, Percy. I don't care how long it takes." Her fist pounds the wood, a heartbeat of its own.

"You don't get to push me away, not when I choose where I stand. Not when I choose who to love and who to protect and who I want to wait for."

"Alyce, please open the door." Percy tries the handle, easing it gently open. He steps into the moonlit room, pauses, takes in Alyce's glistening face, the moon casting her in silver.

Then she is in his arms.

His mouth finds hers and her cheeks are damp with tears. Kissing: salty and sweet and deep. A tonic for his soul. He leans into her. Time is nothing. Her lips are hot and chapped from the heat of the day but to Percy they are soft as silk.

He breaks with a sigh, landing his head on hers, noses a breath apart.

"I'm not pushing you away, Alyce."

"Then stay. Stay with me tonight. Just lay beside me."

Percy shakes his head. "That right is not mine to take. Not tonight at least."

Her grip loosens, she meets his eyes with moon orbs. "I give you the right."

He laughs. "You're pushy, you know that?"

"I know." She sighs, leaning her head on his sternum again, over his heart. His arms wrap her shoulders, his chin on her head. They're quiet for a moment, which might have been eternity. Part of him prays it is. Let me hold her for eternity. Please.

"You have given me new life, Alyce." The words burn, pure, on his tongue. Vibrating through his body, a song he has always known yet never sung. "New faith. You are a light in this darkness I'm terrified to face. You are the sun, encouraging me to grow, pulling away the shadows with a new dawn."

"That's so romantic." She half sobs, trying to tug loose from his grip. "Percy, I need to write it down."

"I'll write it tomorrow."

"You'll forget."

"I won't. For you, I will remember."

Scooping her up, he holds her in his arms, curled like a child in his grip. He sways, humming. Lying her gently on her bed, Alyce snuggles into the covers.

"You'll stay?"

"It's late."

He presses a kiss to her forehead. "Goodnight, Alyce." His eyes trace hers as he backs into the hall, closing her door with a click. He leans against the wood for a moment, breath evening as he listens to his love on the other side.

His heart rate slows, matching hers. The door is a universe between them, the floor his own planet. He is Lor, waiting. Praying for his love to meet him. Willing to cross a galaxy or swim the length of the world, yet he is rooted. Planted into the earth.
She must come to him.

He is sure she sleeps when he rises, down the hall and out the door his feet take him. His mind full.

The gardens are bright, towering trees casting shadows and Percy opens his arms to the Divine. The constant weight in his chest is ebbing slowly out of him. The pain and grief are being washed from his soul and the cleansing ache is wonderful.

With a shaky breath Percy realizes his spirit is at peace.

"Thank you."

xiv.

A bouquet of tiny white blooms rests beside Alyce's bed. Four pointed petals with yellow centers and long green leaves, dark in the sun. She plucks the small note attached to the knotted twine.

Meet me in the gardens.

Her face blooms. Throwing off the bed clothes, she dashes about the room to dress.

The stairs creak and shudder underfoot, an oversized orange skirt tumbles after her.

"Where are you going?" Sol casts her a glance over the morning paper, mossy green brow raised.

Alyce squeals, pulling on boots. "On an adventure. With Percy."

Sol snorts, returning his attention. "Sounds like youngling activities."

"Sol," Alyce buttons her grey shirt, stolen from Percy's closet. "I am older than you, by Alom standards."

Sol gawks at her but she is already out the door, missing his approving grin.

Alyce brushes fingers through her hair, trying hopelessly to keep the tight curls from coiling every direction at once. She fails, resorting to tying the twine from Percy's flowers round her head, trapping the curls between twisted knots.

Percy is waiting under two massive oaks, for once up before her. A long coat sits on his shoulders and dark jeans grab his waist. A white shirt blinding in the morning light.

"Morning." Alyce grins.

"Morning." Percy twirls a pale bloom in his hand, before placing the flower amid her curls. Alyce fingers the silky petals.

"Where are we going?" They walk down the only dirt road, sky still pink and yellow with dawn, the light reflected off his glossy boughs.

"Town." Percy passes her an Afiya bottle, his a pale green, hers emerald as night.

"I wanted to visit some stores, check in on Sol's Afiya shop, he leaves new recipes there, and pass

145

through a few bookstores on our way." He grins.

"Yes!" Alyce sips her breakfast, the dark, earthly moonlight rich and energizing.

They reach the train depot and wait, Percy rocking back and forth on his heels, jingling left over payment chips from the fare. Alyce with nervous hands buried deep in her orange pockets, fingering his note.

Last night still burns between them. She cannot remember falling asleep. Cannot think of much other than his thumb tracing her jaw, her cheek bone, her bottom lip.

The train roars its coming, Alyce startles. Percy laughs when she takes his arm. "This one has a broken muffler. It's only used between Sunstreet and Longdol because Central Ulna Station got complaints about the noise."

"I can see why." Alyce shouts back. She presses her hand to the flower, keeping it in place as the train rolls past.

Passengers exit and others hurry on, Percy taking Alyce's arm as they enter, settling in open window seats.

Announcements on times and stops, the crew feeding the ion engine and then the train is roaring onto its next location.

"It's a half hour ride, much easier than the commute to Central Ulna." Percy stares out the window, the scene a blur of green and blue and growing orange sunlight. Occasionally, there is a darkness, speeding past them like a blink in the light, and Alyce thinks of the Stonefloor. The damage it's caused.

"Why work so far away?"

"Only Halo was willing to take on volunteer nurses."

"Why not work as an actual nurse?"

"I am an actual nurse."

"I mean a paid one."

Percy looks away. "I wanted to feel I was giving something back after the war. Doing good instead of harm. Volunteering seemed the easiest way."

She touches two fingers to his knee, drawing his attention. "You could never do harm."

He grimaces softly. "Parts of me wish that were true." He studies her. "And you, Alyce? What is it you run from?"

She pulls away, hands in her lap. "My father laid out the kind of person he needed me to be. You cannot mold a shape already taken form. I never wanted what he had for me, and I wasn't given a choice." Her voice hardens.

"I can understand that, taking roads you didn't want."

"I moved out, lived with a friend for a while. The war got bad enough we decided to go home. Then the bombs hit Kilo. I don't remember much after that. Until I woke up in Halo Hospital, broken ribs and burn wounds."

She smiles, like that will brush the pain away. She doesn't want to relive the run for her life, the fact she knows Iliana is gone, left her to fend for herself, that she woke up voiceless and alone. She had been voiceless for so long, before she met Percy. Before his words healed her soul.

"How long were you at the hospital, before we met?" His voice is so soft.

"Couple weeks? A month? Closer to two, I think. Sorry." She shakes her head. "It's all kind of a daze. I suppose I would have been given papers if I had discharged like a normal person."

"But you ran instead."

"Yep. I did. That was the last battle, the one in my city."

Percy pales, warm face ashen. "I could see about getting your records, if you would like." He adds softly.

Alyce shakes her head. "It's alright, I don't need them."

Percy takes her hand, squeezes her fingers. "I wish I'd known you were there."

"What do you mean?"

Percy gives her a knowing look. The dots click.

"*You* were there."

Percy presses his lips together. "I was. I lost my brother in that attack."

Alyce is stricken, silent. The loss of a home. The loss of a brother. Loss of freedom. Loss of life.

Alyce grips Percy's hands, brings his fingers to her lips. She kisses each knuckle.

"I was a soldier, Alyce. You know what that means."

"I do. More than you think."

His eyes hold so much pain, Alyce wishes she could take it all away. How can she blame him, as she knows some might do, learning their home was attacked, lives lost, to the man before her. But she cannot find any anger for him, knows it was not by his hands that the city fell.

"I'm sorry, you lost your brother. May the Divine hold him. Both of you."

"I'm sorry you lost a friend. A family. May the Divine guide you."

The train rolls into Longdol station with a clinking hiss. Alyce jostles in her seat, unused to the jolting stops. Percy extends a hand, lifting her up, and doesn't let go as they exit the train, filing through the waiting crowds on cobble stone streets.

The depot falls away, and a town blooms in its wake. Nothing like Central Ulna, with its new buildings and tall towers, glass shining as if trying to hide something. Longdol is old, buildings brick and streets wide and a jostling market lines the main street.

"Here." Percy pulls her toward a stand, steaming with sweet Afiya. Percy pays for an orange bottle, passing it into her hands, now cold in the absence of his. Alyce sniffs.

"It's orange moon Afiya. I've had it once before."

She takes the tiniest sip, then a gulp, the light traveling through her body and into her soul.

"So good!"

"I'm glad you think so. Are you going to share?" He laughs, smile bright as sunlight.

"No." Alyce clutches the bottle to her chest, then releases it with a smile.
Percy downs another portion, and they save the rest for Sol.

"This is my favorite." He sighs. Alyce cleans a bit of Afiya on the corner of his lips.

"Come on." Percy takes her hand again, fingers sticky. The market swirls around them, bodies pressing and shuffling.
Vendors shouting about their wares.

Percy tugs her into a doorway, gladly relieving her from the unfamiliar crush of so many Etz.

"I'm not a fan of crowds." He points into the building. "There's a boutique here. I thought we might find some things for you."

Alyce pushes the door opens, a quiet shop of clothing and jewels and low lights. A woman greets them at the counter. Alyce nods, wanting to slink between the rows instead of drawing attention, but Percy walks up to the counter.

"We're looking for things her size, and...whatever style she likes."

"Percy," Alyce speaks over a row of blouses, "I'll be fine."

He shrugs, thanking the woman, who returns with a sniff to binding chains and gems into jewelry.

Alyce combs through the rows, pulling out slim jeans and a dark jacket that doesn't bear her father's emblem.

"Here." Percy plops a pile of clothing on the chair outside the changing room, running a hand through his hair, golden curls bouncing back into place. Alyce shifts through pale blouses and long skirts, loose jackets and dainty shoes.

"I think I'd prefer boots."

"I can do that. Do you like these?" He gestures to the rest of the pile.

"Some of them." She shrugs. Though wearing a skirt now, (as it was the only thing currently wearable for her) it was a privilege to wear clothing she knew wasn't built for fighting, or running for your life, or surviving a war. These are sundresses and long walks on a beach and harvesting herbs for Afiya in the midday heat. These represented a different part of her. A part she never thought she would be able to choose.

A split second, and Alyce makes a choice about her life. She brings them all into the dressing room.

They leave with a handful of shirts, loose and flowing and pale to protect her from the sun. Two skirts, one dark and thick, another purple and shimmering. And though she told herself no, that she did not need to be a warrior anymore, that she never really was, there are a dark pair of jeans. Thick and capable and perhaps ruining her future of soft days and quiet nights, but she buys them anyway. Swallowing acid out of habit.

She is still her father's daughter. She is still the woman raised to be a warrior, and she cannot yet fathom a life where she is perfectly safe. So she also buys a jacket to accompany it, and Percy says nothing as he pays the bill.

He carries the bag, large enough to fit a child inside, and they emerge fifteen payment chips short.

"You didn't have to do that for me." Alyce suddenly shy.

"Oh, yes, we did. Sol would have my bark if we returned without outfits for you. How long have you been wearing hospital scrubs and makeshift sheets?"

Alyce laughs, trying to remove the bag from his grip. "At least let me carry it."

"Absolutely not. You need to choose the Afiya Sol wants, since you're the one he's training. The shop is just around the corner."

They press through the bodies, keeping to clearer parts of the sidewalk and slipping between open alleys when needed.

"Great thing about little towns, everything is a walk away." Percy winces, as if regretting his words. "Especially when you have stingy folks who don't want to pay train fares unless they have to."

"In the city, everything's walking distance, though the streets weren't always safe. Especially during the war." She grips her fist, then meets his eyes, lightened by the sun. Honey warm and soft.

"How long did you live there?" His voice is so gentle; she is glass he does not wish to break.

"Not long. Sometimes I wish I could go back. There is something like magic, living alongside so many strangers. Each name unknown."

"Until you ask."

"Until I ask."

Alyce smiles, taking his hand. Percy kisses her wrist, heart beating under his lips.

The Afiya shop opens with a bell Percy knocks his head into. The silver instrument tangling in golden curls.

"Ah, sorry!" A girl runs from behind a cluttered worktable, dark braids trailing her blouses purple strings. "I knew I hung that bell too low."

"It's fine." Percy laughs, shaking out his head, curls sticking to his curved boughs, giving him a halo. "You probably don't expect your customers to be so tall."

"Taller customers have passed through without causing a scene." The girl places her hands on her hips, onyx skin winking with light, reflective as glass, holding a dark rainbow within her.

Percy laughs again, rich and deep, wiping his eyes as he turns to her.

"Alyce, this is Anya, Sol's niece."

"Wonderful to meet you…" The girl grips her hand, finally noticing her, her face freezing over as she takes Alyce in.

"Yes…" Alyce starts, her eyes widening with fear. She remembers the healer in the cellar, the only one who would bandage her wounds after her father's training. The only one who didn't blame her for not being Yahalom.

The girl had disappeared when Sol left Radius for the first wave of war. She must have accompanied him. Alyce wonders if she recognizes her.

"You are Alom." Is all Alyce can pull from her lips, praying her fear looks like shock. Praying the girl does not give away who she is. What she still has to do.

"Yep." Anya twirls from them, either hiding Alyce's identity or oblivious, she cannot be sure. "What can I help you find?"

"First, this is from Sol." Percy pulls rumpled paper from his coat. "New recipes. And he promises more on the way."

"Perfect." Anya rummages through her worktable and Alyce peruses the shelves.

Jasmine Afiya, pale and delicate, with whorls in the milky broth like suns.

River Afiya, rushing through its bottle as if the glass never held it.

New moon bottles, inky black flecked with silver starlight.

Alyce pulls one from the shelf as Anya passes Percy a wad of payment chips. "Tell Sol I said hi."

"Will do." Percy nods, tucking away the chips. "See anything you like?"
Alyce shakes her head. "What am I supposed to be looking for?"

"Most of the recipes are Sol's, if you didn't know. He does my experimenting. The shop is in his name, but I run most of it. Running a business..." Anya rubs her shoulder. "Yeah...it's fun."

"You say that like a burden."

Anya shrugs, shuffling through her loose papers and tools Alyce already recognizes for harvesting ions and packaging Afiya.

"Sometimes I wish there were other things for me, something adventurous. But the Divine knows," she winks. "I just keep making plans, waiting for one to be approved. Now what can I help you find?"

Alyce waits for her voice to hold an edge of familiarity. For Anya to tell Percy who she really is. Sol settled in Ulna for a different life, maybe Anya did too. Maybe she doesn't want to remember.

Maybe Alyce should play along, if it means one day she might forget too.

"Something Sol doesn't know how to make, to challenge him."

"I have just the blend." Then the adorable girl cackles, and Alyce wishes she hadn't asked.

They're given a large bottle, the blend inky green. Heavenly fumes rise from its opened top.

"I found this at the market, one of a kind. I haven't cracked the ingredients yet. Tell him he has one week to get me its recipe."

"How long have you been studying it?" Percy peers into its depth, the Afiya casting emerald light onto his hands.

"Two months."

"Two months!?" Alyce and him speak in unison. Percy slips the cap carefully back into place.

"He wanted a challenge, he'll appreciate my thought." She winks. "It's sure to be a bestseller. An Afiya for grounding and quiet wonder, they are rare to find."

"We'll be sure to pass that on." Alyce tucks the Afiya in their bag, nestled safely amid the clothing.

"Thank you, Anya. Sol is stopping by next, but he's to send word when he's coming." Percy says.

"Only with that recipe." Anya tucks her hands on her hips, studying them.

This is it, Alyce fears. She will tell Percy she is the daughter of Jaal, leader of the Diamond Guard. He will know-

"You two are cute." Anya chirps.

"Thanks."

"We are?" His voice squeaks, surprised.

Alyce jabs out her elbow, making Percy welp.

He grins.

Her cheeks burn bright red.

The bookshop is quiet when they enter, fingers intwined. Percy doesn't release her hand as he pours over the shelves, poetry and lore and histories kissed by his touch. Dust lifts in his wake.

Alyce tugs a large tome from the shelf, flipping through gleaming illustrated poetry and ancient fairy tales. She traces an indented image of a large laurel tree, roots twisting off the page, boughs holding too many leaves to count. The face of a boy stares up at her. Suddenly she can see the places feet would have stood, his carved jaw and raised hands, coaxing down the moon. She flips the page, delight bubbling from her mouth.

"It's the Woman on the Moon. The story you told me!" She holds up the book.

Percy peeks up from tiny, handwritten notebooks. "So it is." The book closes in his hand. He takes the tome with care, their fingers brushing.

"My mother always told me this story; said it was important." He traces the letters hanging in the starry air between the lovers, pages torn from their hearts and given form.

"I've been told that Nadala remained in Radius, which was how she survives the pressure of the ocean depths, because the sea gave her what she needed to become diamond. Diamonds are not born; they must be forged. Yahalom we call them."

"The Divine's Stone."

Alyce takes back the book. "I've never thought about the name like that. Thank you, Percy. That made my heart happy."

They walk the length of each shelf, touching each spine and whispering titles like prayers. The tome never leaves Alyce's tucked embrace, and Percy gathers a variety of notebooks, searching her approval for each one.

Snuggling in two large chairs, they read and pass poetry back and forth. A tall window casts fading warmth, lighting their features in gold. Percy finally taps her hand, signaling time to go.

They reach the counter with soft poems and notebooks and the tome of fairy tales, their arms full. A tired boy adds their total.

"That will be a hundred and four chips-"

"A hundred-" Percy's face blanches. The boy holds up the tome, "this is an original, hand painted, with orally collected stories."

Percy turns to Alyce, nervous. "I can't afford that." He whispers.

"It's alright." She pats his hand. "I have the only storyteller I need."

She gives one long look at the gilded frame, the boy tucking it on a shelf behind the counter.

"I'm sorry, Alyce. It is beautiful." Percy pays for their notebooks and poems. "I think my mother told other stories from that book, maybe I could remember some."

"Perhaps your mother was one of the contributors." The bell jingles behind them, the evening air warm and blissful, fresh with night.

"It's alright, Percy. I am excited to hear more of these tales."

His face brightens and they walk toward the depot.

Tickets and waiting and gripping Percy's arm as the train comes rumbling in for the evening travelers.

They sit in a lone booth, framed with setting, golden light. The sky falling toward pinks and turquoise blues.

"I can't remember a day that felt so...normal."

"It's normal to take all day shopping sprees with strange men?" Percy arches a perfect brow.

"It's normal to go on a date with someone you're interested in."

"Is that what we are? Interested?"

"I am." Her cheeks burn. "I meant what I said last night, Percy. I've never met anyone like you, and I want to be someone in your life. As long as I can."

"I'm teasing." He takes her hand, tugs on dark fingers. Their skin night and day, laughing and cherished, their hands the sky.

"I meant what I said, too. Sometimes..." he bows his head. "I have this fear inside me still. Fear something will happen to you, me, everyone I care about. That I will be alone again. I know that sounds selfish and probably stupid; the Divine has work to do for me to be the man I was again."

"Maybe you are meant to be someone new now. Someone who has lived the life you have and still chooses grace. Chooses healing. You cannot control the things that turn you about like a storm, but you can choose how you let the effects playout. How you react. See these moments as opportunities and ask the Divine to shape you instead of struggling with your own two hands."

Percy brings her fingers to his lips, kisses her. "I love you."

She lays a hand on his head, buries her fingers in sunlit curls. "I know."

They curl together on the bench, his arm round her waist, her head on his chest. The sun has fallen, and night rises in hues of blue and navy and pale yellow.

"Are you asleep?" Percy traces a thumb down her cheek.

"Nope." Alyce says, yawning, eyes still closed. "Are we home?"

"We are. Home." Percy says the word like a prayer and Alyce feels it in her chest.

"Are you forgetting your promise?" Soft and familiar and shaking her awake, the voice comes.

As pious and faithful as she chooses to be, Alyce pushes the words away. *"She left me, what was I to do? Please, I do not want to leave him."*

A quiet hum. *"Perhaps you were meant to come here. But there are still things I have asked of you. Do you still listen to My Word?"*

"Ask, and I will follow. I am Your stone."

Percy takes her hand, guiding her home, where the warm lights of Sol's kitchen wait for them.

"This is for you." Percy presses a paper into her hand, shadows of the porch hiding their faces. Alyce unfurls it with a smile.

You plant new life in me.

New faith. New stories.

You are a light in the darkness,

The sun,

Encouraging growth.

You pull me from the shadows,

Gifting a new dawn.

I bloom in your presence

and long for you to do the same.

I long to hold you on late nights,

Head heavy on my heart.

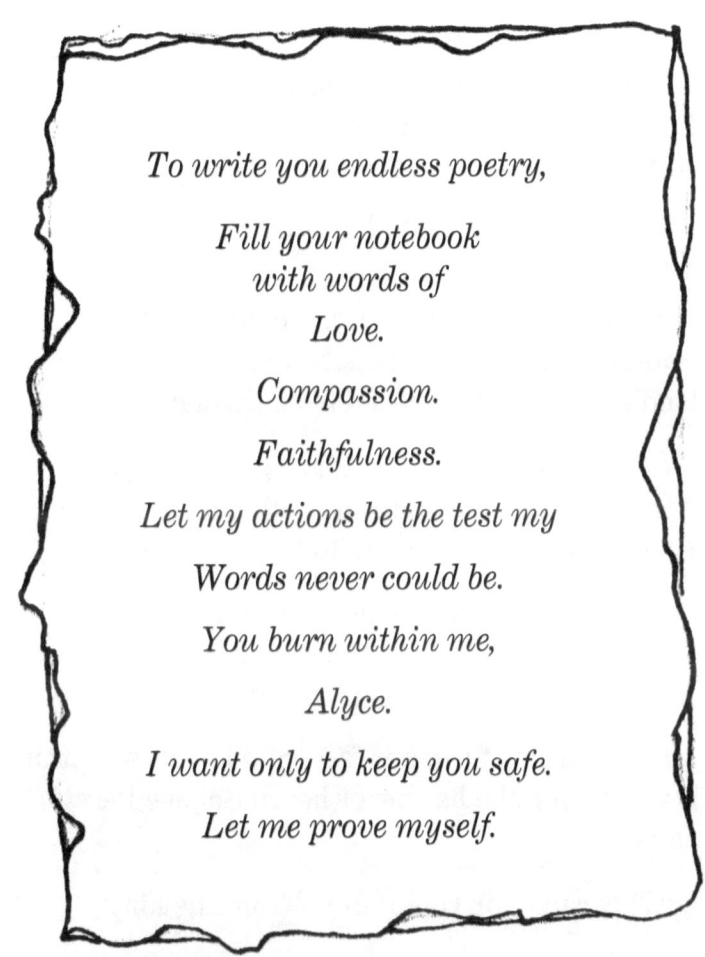

To write you endless poetry,

*Fill your notebook
with words of
Love.*

Compassion.

Faithfulness.

Let my actions be the test my

Words never could be.

You burn within me,

Alyce.

I want only to keep you safe.

Let me prove myself.

Her eyes glisten and burn.
"You always make me cry, Percy Waiden."

"Perhaps you need to, Alyce Chime."

She shakes her head, rising onto her toes, pressing
her lips to his.

They spill laughing into the foyer, boots and creaking floors and giggles. Alyce kisses him once more, tasting Afiya, sweet and rich on her tongue.

Percy sheds his coat, depositing their bag on the floor.

Percy wraps his arms around her waist, they waddle together into the kitchen, their labradorite landlord coming ash faced from the hall.

Sol's stare burns into a glaring white paper waiting on the table. He sits with a sigh, the chair about to give out, holding hundreds of pounds.

Alyce cannot see a General from the Radian army, only a tired man, one who holds out the crisp sheet and Alyce catches a flash of the seal.

Blood drains from her face. She knows something is wrong, for she has never heard Sol use Percy's name.

"This came for you, Percy. From the king."

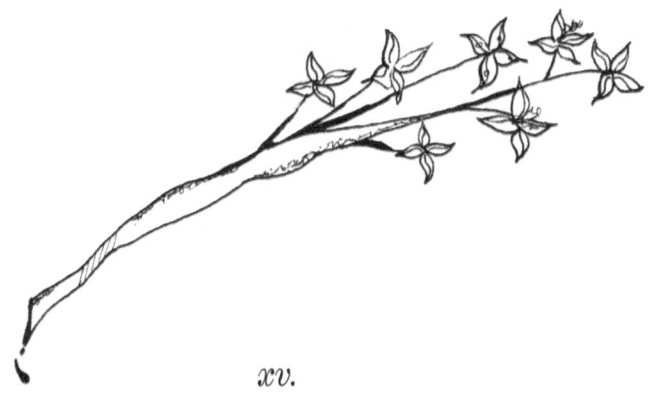

xv.

Alyce stiffens under his touch.

Percy swallows, pushing, shoving, fighting like a dying man the panic oozing into his blood.

He keeps a tight hold on his breath, forcing even lungfuls to fill and empty, even as they leave his mouth with a tremor. Alyce's grip on him tightens, grounding.

"Let me see." Percy holds out a hand, thanking the Divine it doesn't shake. He scans the script, the fluid lines, the golden sun seal, points like knives driving across the page and into his brain.

"The King has sent for me." He all but collapses into a chair, Alyce supporting his arm. He doesn't let go of her hand, Sol eyes their entwined fingers.

"To reward me, he says, for finding his son. It isn't a request." He tosses the paper, or imagines he does. Imagines defying the person responsible for his brother's death. It was not Radius who started this war. Not Radius who called for untrained soldiers to fight, only to watch them burn in the fires of the Sun King himself. Who kept his own son a secret because of a ruined face. Percy can only imagine how Prince Rae's scars came into being.

166

But the paper is still in his hands, he hasn't let go, and he is looking hopelessly at Sol.

"You have to go." The older man says. "Its an order."

"I know." Percy squeezes his eyes shut.

"I will go with you." Alyce sits next to him. "It will be alright."

"I know," he releases a shuddering sigh. "I just need a moment." The creak of a chair, then his feet on the stairs, then the darkness of his room and the click of his door. Percy leans against the wood, breath deep and uneven and trembling hands wrack his curls into poof.

He waits for the panic to stop, the anxiety running through his arteries to rest. He waits for a long time.

"Percy?"

Alyce. Knocking on his door, revealing the light of the hall and her worried features.

"Hey." He's slumped by his desk, paper scattered and inked under his elbow. His spider plant has a soothing tendril wrapped around one finger.

She passes him a warm cup of Afiya, curling into his favorite cushioned seat, flicks on his solar lamp, the ion buzzing in a blue glass jar.

"Want to talk?" She takes a sip.

Percy sighs, leaning back in his chair. "No. Not about that." He takes her hand, an honest grin touching his cheeks. "I had fun today. More than I've had in a while."

"Mh." She says into her cup, one eye lifting to him. "Maybe I'm good for you."

"Or maybe I'm just susceptible to cute girls."

She spits into her cup, laughing. Percy grins with her and by the Divine, this feels right.

She feels right.

She was always meant to be right next to his soul. Rested and protected between his clavicle and ribs. She is meant to be a part of him.

He leans forward. Takes her hand. "Alyce." His thumb rubbing circles on her ebony dark skin. "You don't have to come. I know you ran after the King arrived. I know he came with people from your homeland, and if I'm right, you didn't want to be spotted."

Her grip on him tightens. "Jasmine threatened me, trying to force me out. She was going to tell the King, and my father."

He winces at the thought, but her words draw him back to her.

"I didn't want to lose you. I made a choice." She looks down. "I chose running over being found by my father." She shakes her head. "At least I knew where you worked, I would have found you again." Her voice cracks. "But you came for me." Crystal tears drop onto their joined hands.

Percy's hand finds her zygomatic bone, pinky finger cupping the curve of her jaw. Her eyes are twin moons, cast in blue and yellow from his light. "I would have traveled to Radius if I knew you were forced to return. I would have come for you. After my panic attack, of course."

"Right." She hiccups, smile slow and damp. He wipes an errant tear, another falling into its place. Percy leans forward, kissing the tears from her cheeks. His mouth travels downward, hovering a fingers breath from her lips. This kiss is tender. Gentle and floating, fireflies in his chest. She leans into him, deepening their connection.

"I don't want to lose you, Alyce."

"Never."

Neither notice the quiet footsteps in the hall, the shadow lingering under the door. Sol's sigh is heavy and pained.

Rae wakes with a muffled scream.

Gold sheets strangle him. Silver bells hanging from his bed are screams repeating in his head.

A maid scurries over, hands nervous. She's too young to stay up all night, to keep him from dreaming.

Maybe he should have taken his father's sleeping draft. He swears, chest heaving.

"I just need a moment." He gasps out, monsters still roaming through his mind, his words. He doesn't trust himself.

"Of course, your highness. I am here when you need me."

"Fetch Flyn, then go."

The girl bows again, hands trembling. He should be gentler, watch his tone, take the Divine-forsaken tonic. Maybe kindness just isn't on the list today, not with what he needs to do.

The maid leaves and he lies back in bed with a sigh, running trembling fingers over his scarred face. Groaning, he rolls, taking the tonic from his bedside and swallowing two droppers full.

It burns down his throat and Rae breathes through the sickening taste, counting to ten. Twenty. Fifty. Releasing a breath, the effects take hold, his mind softened, the ache of burnt skin lessened.

He rises, throwing on a robe, embroidered with gems and gold silk. The doors open unceremoniously and Rae smirks as a disheveled youth prances into his rooms. Eyes lined with coal and hair spiked atop his head. The dress is casual, but in a 'I'm rich and life-friend of the Prince' kind of way. A half looped tie and sleek vest drape over dark leather pants.

Flyn grins.

"What mischief are we achieving today, your highness?"

Rae slips on his mask, cold and metal, hiding his scars. "I don't know." He sighs, tossing off his robe for loose tops and sword belts and dress pants. He needed to look somewhat presentable. "Have anything in mind?"

Rae arches a brow, though Flyn cannot see his face. Just his eyes, blue as day, and a wicked curve to the right side of his mouth. He powders his boughs, dark with black dust, lines the uneven edges in gold. A single chain is looped from his good ear up to the top of his right bough, dainty and gold. He studies his features for a moment, the aura of a prince he places on his head everyday. He has no other choice.

"We could terrorize the kitchen staff, steal melted Afiya. Race equines through the woods. Look up more pictures of your future bride." Flyn wiggles his eyebrows.

"Don't remind me." Rae turns from the mirror. Pulls a glove over his ruined hand. Flexes his fingers, joints popping.

"I was thinking of hitting things a little higher today."

"So bombing the barracks. Dyeing the washing-"

"No. All the way up." Rae grins ruefully. "We're seeing my father."

The court room is blinding. Sunlamps line the walls in gilded sconces, casting light a thousand different directions. The Sun King glows on his throne like dying rays of light. Reds and golds and ochers.

Guards and nobles turn their heads, the Radius ambassador casts a long, judging glance. Rae holds his head high, tall boughs twisting from his head, dark as the mask on his face. The silks and velvets dark as night and new moons. He drips disdain and what he hopes is power. His father barely offers a glance.

"King Silver is adamant you offer entry to her. She claims you hold her daughter hostage." The Radius ambassador quips, raising his head before the Ulnain King.

"If I had the Princess in my clutches I wouldn't need you here, now would I?" Usis arches a brow. "I destroyed one of my own cities searching for her. The girl doesn't want to be found."

Rae stands firm, hands clasped behind his back, silently praising the girl. Who would want to be found by Usis?

His skin aches.

"If Princess Iliana is not found by King Silver's arrival, she will invade. With an army." The Radius ambassador's voice rings loud, bitter with tension.

Rae shifts, Usis finally clasping eyes with his son. The Sun King smiles. Panic spikes down his spine. Rae regrets his decision to come. Wishing he had written to his father on these matters instead. But this is why he dressed, lined his scarred eyes with coal, painted himself like a shadow who has never felt pain.

The treaty will be lost if Princess Iliana is not found. He is the reason she is missing, after all. He swears under his breath, taking steady, slow steps toward his father's raised hand.

Usis's eyes glow gold, then white hot.

As much as he hates this, he will not let his people fall back into war. Not after he has seen the horrors it spreads.

"Prince Raedyn will go and seek out his future bride."
The threat is there, even if no one else can see it.

Rae sneers, lifting his chin. "Perhaps she doesn't want to marry."

"Perhaps her opinion does not matter." Usis shoots back. "She will be found, ambassador, I will make sure of it."

The Radius ambassador bows his head once, tilting, almost jeeringly toward the Sun King. Usis lets the taunt go unharmed.

The guards file out, the servants and nobles, until it is only Flyn, Rae, and Usis.

"Flyn, you may go." The Sun King watches the boy bow once, cast a glance toward his son, and walk toward the door as if he owns the palace.

Rae rolls his eyes, trying to warn off this anger inside him. The panic.

"And how, father, do you wish me to find a girl who has been missing for three months?"

The King shrugs, a terrifying move, as his hands curl into fists on his throne. Rae feels the room heat.

"Coincidence. Must be. That's the same amount of time you've been missing, son."

"I've been in the hospital!" Rae shouts. "In case you forgot."

"And the three weeks before that? You were missing then."

Rae curls his fists, mimicking his father; terrifying. Rae refuses to be a mirror. Refuses to succumb. Refuses to let the monsters win.

Usis pulls something from his coat, flicking the folded page open before Rae. "This is your handwriting. Your seal. Your words. Shall I read them?"

Rae cannot object and Usis has already started speaking.

"*-I know we have never met, but I need you to trust me. Don't come here. Don't agree to the marriage. This kingdom is not safe under Usis' rule and never will be. I advise you run, if Radius will not listen to reason. I will meet you in Kilo-*'"

Usis looks over the tattered page. "The last city I burned."

"Searching for me? Or your dignity?"

The temperature grows, now stifling. Rae struggles to breathe, his skin burns beneath his clothing.

Usis stands, and it is a sun gone supernova walking toward him. Usis's own skin smokes with the effort of his powerplay. The Sun King will not burn forever. This is the only thing that gives Rae hope. Someday, he will be free.

Rae's knees fail him, he claws at his throat, the skin scorched from the inside out. Usis bows before his son, takes the masked face in his hand, fingers sinking into the metal, white hot.

"You will find this girl, or I won't leave you with that pretty mouth to speak, or these hands to write. Understand?"

Rae nods, tasting blood. Usis smiles, releasing his son, the heat fades and Rae curls gasping on the palace floor.

"Good." The Sun King exits with a flourish of smoldering silks, Rae's shirt all but burnt from his skin.

Rae pulls the smelting mask from his face, his scars screaming as he gasps for air. Flyn curses when he enters the room. Lifting Rae from the floor, Flyn guides him to a window he throws open.

"Someday, Rae, I'm not going to be able to contain myself. How can he do this to you, his heir? His son?"

"Usis doesn't care, as long as he gets his way." Rae coughs, blood flecking his gloved hand. Flyn rubs a hand along his spine.

"I'll be okay." Rae reassures him, voice hoarse.

"I'm still searching for a healer, someone we can actually trust. All of the court physicians are under your father's thumb."

"I know. I'm just worried about Iliana. I don't know how much time I can give her. He wants me to search for her." Rae grimaces, straightening.

"You'll have to send for her. We're out of time."

"Father is having a ball, to announce my engagement. She'll return by then, I'm sure of it." Rae closes his eyes.

"She'll have to, or there will be none of you to return to."

Rae lifts his eyes to the sun, the mangled skin of his face soft and glimmering. The beauty of new growth and pain of old wounds.

Rae opens his hand, a small white flower blooming from his palm. Vines creep around his temples, looping his forehead in a mock crown. Flowers and roots push from his skin, blooming in red and purples and yellows over his nose. His body an earth.

He finds relief from the stinging pain of new growth, his royal blood containing the gifts of his mother. Flowers grow from his skin, opening pollen filled faces, lifting toward the sun. Roots wrap his fingers, ring his arms. Leaves poke from his skin, giving him wolf hackles along his spine.

"Your skill is growing."

Onol rests beside him on the bench, navy robes near black in the full sun. Stubbed boughs rest nestled in her dark hair, hidden by her looping braid.

"It's easier when I am at peace." Rae releases his hold on the blooms, letting petals fall from his skin and roots retract into his soul. "I am grateful my gift resembles mother's over father's."

"The Bloom and the Sun." Onol recites, twin blue eyes locking on his. "Think of all the good the sun could be, if he learned to withhold the burn of his heat."

"I would prefer being cast into eternal night then endure this." Rae points to his face with his mangled hand. His sister lifts her gaze to the high sun, relishing its heat. Rae catches sight of her burnt boughs, poking through her braid.

Their father is a monster.

"I don't know what you have planned, Rae." Onol meets his eyes. "The Divine tells me it will soon come to pass. You must prepare." Onol rises, Rae catches her hand.

"Do you know?" Voice low. Hollow. *Terrified.*

Onol smiles.

"Long live the Flower King." She whispers, slipping down the garden path, toward the Temple. Rae watches his sister disappear, then buries his head in his hands.

Alyce's muttering breath causes the glowing ion light to waver. It bends under the force of her prayer, threatening to extinguish.

"I thank You, Divine, for Your truth. Your rest. Your divine timing. I thank You, Divine, for my voice, in all its forms. Let it always be a voice of Yours."

Alyce's voice stills, feeling the Divine presence with her. The soft hand on her shoulder.

"How long will you wait? How long will you run?"

She starts to shake. "I know the things You have asked of me. I know there is a reason I met Percy. Oh, there are so many reasons." She smiles, whispering.

"I don't want to leave him."

"Oh, daughter." The feel of warm love covers her. *"Follow My word. I do not leave you."*

Alyce shoves tangling coils from her face, long in the three months away from the Radius Guard. She stands, paces, then returns to the edge of her bed, head bowed.

She's packed before the soft knock comes, jeans and concealing tops and her boots waiting to carry her to Central Ulna. Her jacket the top of the pile. She leaves her skirts, reminders of brighter days.

"It's Sol."

"Come in." Alyce ties up her curls, twine looped between expert fingers. Sol enters, closing the door behind him.

"Where's Percy?"

"On an errand for a patient. Mabel." Sol clenches his hands. Alyce cannot remember if she has ever seen him nervous.

"What's wrong?" Alyce sits.

"I know what you are, Alyce. What you claimed to run from. I'm not sending you away-" He holds up a blue grey hand, reassuring her. "I know you and Percy have grown close, and I'm happy for him, you seem like the kind of girl he needs." His eyes meet hers, suddenly fierce. "But are you going to hurt him? Are you going to lie to him? To me? Because whatever you claimed to be finished with, it's come looking for you."

Sol tosses a crumpled paper into her lap. Alyce unfolds last week's newspaper, searching the pages, scanning columns of weather forecasts and Stonefloor updates and- there, in tiny script, is a small inscription in Radian, sending Alyce's blood running cold.

A,

the morning dove coos,

calling for its love.

The sun answers,

for it knows the dove is alone.

"Underneath, I am still a Radian General. I know what this means. When were you going to tell him someday you would leave?" Sol's hands are shaking. Alyce sinks into the mattress.

"When did this come?"

"Last week."

"You kept this from me?"

"You're not the one who gets to accuse here. When were you going to tell him you've been on a mission this whole time?!"

"Soon." Alyce snaps. Lowering her voice, "I didn't want to lose him, Sol. I can't."

"Above all, Percy values truth. Trust. You have lied to us both."

Dinner is quiet. Percy relays the trials of the day, voice tired as he tries to fill the void of silence. Marred, half moon eyes cast questioning glances to her, but Alyce never responds, keeping her eyes down. She doesn't trust them to keep her secrets.

Sol keeps the conversation going, discussing the Afiya shop, Anya, the latest batch he has yet to crack.

Alyce doesn't speak. What could she say? Nothing Sol will not judge her for, and Percy will not soon learn.

She cannot keep this from him. Not forever, even though she tries. By the Divine, she wanted to try.

Pushing from the table, she leaves early. Percy rises, opening his mouth to speak, but Sol stops him.

"Give her space."

Percy doesn't come to her door, though she waits for him. She doesn't leave her room and worry eats inside her. This is not the daughter her father raised, not the woman she chose to be. Not how she wishes to stand. Yet she cannot move. Cannot stand. Cannot bring herself to find him, for if she sees him- alone- she will tell him. Everything. Hold nothing back, even her betrayal. And she cannot, not yet.

She only wanted a few more days, she prays. A few more days to be with him. To smile. Because when she tells him, she will have to disappear.

"I do not want to disappear. I want to be the sun."

Her tears slip and she lets them fall. "Did I run from You? Or did I run from who I was before?" She asks the Divine. "I was so tired of orders and rules and being a soldier. I wanted *life*. But did I choose wrong? Should I have returned? I don't know what You are going to say, but if You tell me this was wrong, Percy was wrong, I'm going to fight You. As much as I love You, I will fight for him. For us."

"I know, love."

A dove calling out, the sun responding because her love is not to be found. It's code.

Alyce replays the haunting words in her head. She knows what they mean. Her charge is alone, and searching for her. Asking for her return, because the dove cannot reach the height of the heavens, the sun must go to her.

Alyce slips on her boots, grabbing her pack, she takes one last loving glance at the room so much joy has been shared in.

She won't see it again.

Percy grins, shyly, as she comes down the stairs. "You don't have to come with me." He's giving her a chance to stay. To keep life simple. To be safe. Alyce shakes her head.

"I will follow you anywhere."

Sol sighs in quiet exasperation from the kitchen. Alyce steps away when Percy leans in with a kiss.

Neither speak.

"Well," Percy blinks. "We cannot miss this train. It will be a long ride."

Alyce shoulders her pack, lifting Percy's too. "You had better say goodbye, I'll wait for you outside."

Percy nods, heading into the kitchen. Alyce doesn't linger outside the door, doesn't want to hear what will be spoken.

The air is cool, crisp, kissing her cheeks. Wind pulls her dark coils, and Alyce fights them from her face. She needed a haircut. She needed more courage. She needed several things, some she was too afraid to grasp.

Percy practically bounces down the front steps, as if they were taking a honeymoon and not meeting the vicious Sun King and his demands.

Still, it is this grin she has fallen in love with. Given up everything for.

Almost everything.

Her faith keeps her anchored and moving forward. Even if that means different paths. She locks on brown eyes. Leans forward. Kisses him.

"What is that for?" Percy smiles, taking their bags. She shakes her head, forcing a smile, praying it is believable.

"I love you. There needs to be a reason?"

"I guess not." Percy loops an arm around her waist, tugs her to him. His kiss is deeper and Alyce feels her eyes burn.

She will miss him.

More than anything.

They release; Alyce comes down from her tiptoes. "Percy..." She grips the front of his shirt, fingers trembling.

Sol stands, arms crossed, on the porch.

"Let's talk on the train." She tugs his hand, heading toward the station.

Tickets paid for with the King's seal. Luxury seats taken. Their bags stored away, only a few books Percy snagged and two pens Alyce kept in her pocket for company.

They are silent as the train pulls from Sundol Station, and Alyce takes in every color and inch of land, afraid this is her last time.

If she speaks, she will tell him. So she doesn't speak. Couldn't if she wanted to. They watch the land pass in a blur of silence neither breaks, as if Percy can read her thoughts. Knows she needs this time to process.

There is a tap on her leg, Alyce startles.

"Need something for your thoughts?" He passes her a notebook, takes one of her pens.

Is this what life between them would look like? Give and take and balance.

Suddenly the silence doesn't matter, because if these are really their last days together, then she will spend it in smiles and laughter and a warm glow to remember on nights she will spend alone.

"Write me a poem, and I'll do the same."

"A challenge. Taken." Percy grins, kissing her hand.

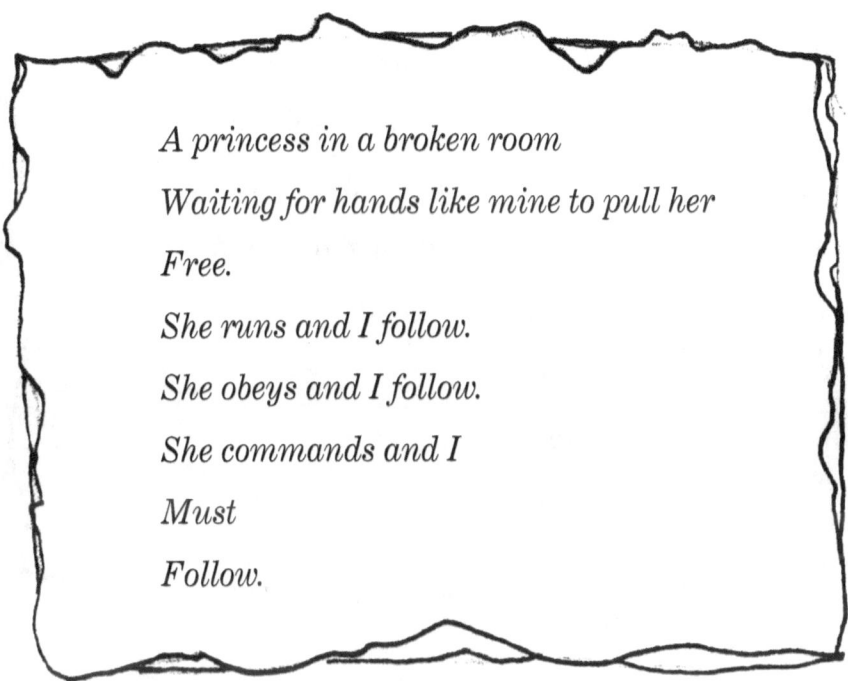

A princess in a broken room
Waiting for hands like mine to pull her
Free.
She runs and I follow.
She obeys and I follow.
She commands and I
Must
Follow.

She's shy, passing it to Percy. Every word true.

Are you a caged bird,
Sitting all alone.
Open your eyes,
Dear one.
The sun calls for you
The rain chases you
The moon kisses you and

I imagine I am the moon.
My heart is wild, You are
an anchor. My soul
trembles, You are only soft
hands, Loving me.
You run?
I follow.
Always.

Now he is shy, as words are passed between them.

They exchange pieces of their souls for scraps of torn pages, words in exchange for feeling. For memory. For moments in time past and time to come.

They write until their hands ache and then they write until their fingers are dark with ink.

Finally, pages in, she stops. Percy meets her gaze, grins slowly, taps the seat beside himself.

"Come rest. You'll need your fighting energy for the King."

She arches a brow. "Is that a joke?"

"Maybe. Just come here." He opens his arm, Alyce snuggles onto his bench. His arm drapes her shoulder, fingers running sparks across her skin.

"Let me tell you a story." He whispers into her hair.

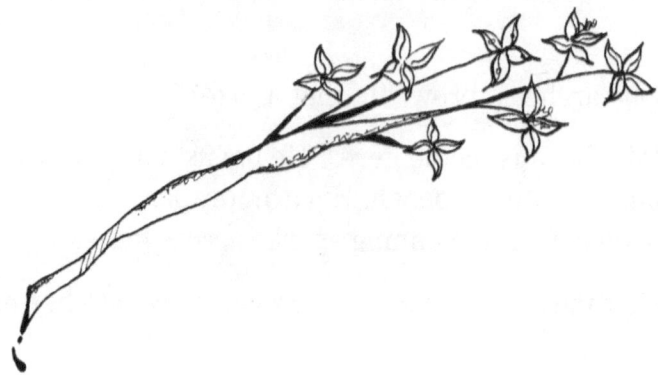

xviii.

The train pulls into the King's private station, gilded walls and glass ceilings. Electric wires jolting both of their frequencies as they step off. Hundreds of people mill around, nobles and the rich, servants and those looking to level up their status.

Percy grips Alyce's hand, and they wait beside the track.

"Mr. Waiden?" A snub looking Etz man sniffs, taking in their rugged appearance with looping green eyes. His coat gleams in the late afternoon sun and polished boughs rise from his head.

Percy nods his head, holding out a hand the man doesn't take. He locks eyes on Alyce, taking in her lack of Etz energy and the missing boughs from her head.

"This is my dear friend, Alyce Chime. She will be accompanying me."

"Just so." The man claps, and two boys come forward from the crowd, taking their luggage in gloved hands.

Percy starts to protest, but the man gives him a hard stare. His hands start to shake, Alyce takes one, entwining their fingers.
Percy smiles down at her.

"I shall escort you to the palace and ensure you are presentable for the royal engagement ball. It is there the King intends to meet you."

"Perfect." Alyce answers as they press through the crowds. Or rather the crowds shift for them. The man eyes her again; Percy's hand tightens on hers.

"I was unaware you were bringing a guest, Mr. Waiden. I shall have to prepare an extra room."

"I'm sure you are an expert in such matters." Percy forces a bright smile. "It will be no trouble getting us rooms beside one another."

The man pauses. "Indeed."

They board a motorized carriage and Alyce is in awe of the electricity, power from the King's own body, running through the machine, though her teeth buzz as it rumbles over the streets and the odd frequency has her on edge.

Percy grips the bottom of his seat with white hands.

The palace is a looming tower of gold, extending high over Ulna city. Courts and open aired halls curve around it's points and loop around the base in a maze of buildings.

Percy doesn't think of his brother, doesn't think of their parents, doesn't think of ruined cities and how close Alyce and him had come to being enemies.

He only thinks of her hands in his, her warmth beside him. This will sustain him, in a land growing unstable and dark.

Their guide ushers them through doors and up a long case of stairs. Past rooms of glass walled gardens and halls of gold.

A man walks toward them, high boughs regal and draped in gold chains. A mask of ivory covering his face.

"Frederik." The Prince greets respectfully to him. "Where are you taking them?"

"The east wing, your highness. They requested rooms close together and there is only one ready for Mr. Waiden in the south courters. I know this is against protocol."

The Prince waves a gloved hand. "Nothing is too much for the man who rescued me." His masked gaze slips to Percy, then to Alyce. His eyes widen.

"I would like to greet them, properly, while you ready the rooms."

"Sire, the rooms are-"

"Find one that is joint. And you will need a supply of moon Afiya, it seems. Take what you need from Princess Iliana's rooms. She has no need of them."

"Yes, sire." Frederik bows, taking his leave.

Prince Rae extends a hand to a nearby door. "Let me offer you some refreshments, it is the least I could do."

Percy has a hand on Alyce's shoulder, trying hard not to let her know it trembles. They wait for Prince Rae to sit, then near collapse on the sofa, as if they haven't been traveling for hours.

Rae claps and crystalized Afiya is set before them in glittering arrays of yellow and ruby and midnight blue.

Rae takes one of the navy ones, popping it into his mouth. Percy grabs a yellow, if only to loosen his nerves.

"How are you feeling, your highness?" He asks, examining the Prince as he would any patient.

Rae shrugs. "Well enough. I didn't realize you would be attending." While the Prince's voice is casual, his gaze keeps slipping to Alyce. Eyes piercing and starbright blue through the swirl of ivory mask. The chains hum as he shifts.

"I trust you received the threatening message from my father." Again, eyes toward Alyce, who is studying her clasped hands.

Percy shifts on the sofa. "I did."

Prince Rae locks his gaze on him. "You were a soldier in my father's army."

"I was."

"Did you know he destroyed Kilo himself?" Rae tuts, as if this were a misfortunate passing matter, and not the lives of thousands on one man's hands. On his father's hands.

Lightning strikes his core. "My brother died in that attack. We were told it was a new bomb from Radius."

"A bomb with the power of the sun." Rae leans back, voice taunt. "If Radius had that kind of power, we would never have gone to war. I know what you are thinking, Alyce." Rae's eyes shift to her, soften. "If Usis could create destruction like that, why not end the war from the very start? I will tell you." He leans forward, takes one of her hands.

Percy's stomach tightens.

"Usis wanted war. Wanted the Stonefloor." Rae continues. "Wanted an excuse for his new electricity to be pumped into every home and person. I have been his test subject these long years. I bear the scars of his success. The proof of his ability to harness his own power and preserve it." He pulls back, Alyce grips her fist.

"Why are you telling us this?" Percy stands.

Prince Rae opens his arms. "A friendly warning. I owe you my life, you were my nurse. And you, Miss Chime. I heard every poem and story you read to me. I heard every word spoken in that room, humming from your lips. I mean to thank you."

Alyce rises. "No need, your majesty. I have all that I need."

"Good." The Prince grins.

"I shall see you both at the ball. The maid shall show you where to go."

They bow, taking their leave. A turn and a turn and a new court entirely. They almost dance through twisting halls and dark secrets. Finally they reach their rooms, a quiet hall baring their doors. Percy pauses outside his own.

"What use would the Prince have telling us that?" His voice hushed.

"Perhaps," Alyce takes a step forward, folding her hands over his. "He is asking for help. He was a child, and his father experimented on him. We know the King's electricity is harmful, this only proves it."

"I agree, the Prince does need help."

Her eyes lighten, just a touch.

"He needs a counselor and healing Afiya and the Divine to touch his life."

She smiles, but it is almost disappointed. "I agree, Percy." She takes a step back. "We should rest. I'll see you tonight."

"Tonight."

Alyce shuts her door, yet Percy remains in the hall, the feeling of paper still ghosting his hands.

Alyce had been given a note.

A maid knocks on the gilded door, bearing a tray for supper. Percy rises from the cushioned floor beside the bed, greeting her with a small smile and thanking her.

His room is spacious, carved décor and rich curtains, a bed the size of three and a seating area beside a balcony overlooking the main city. There is also a door he hasn't touched, leading to a room beside his own. It's all Percy can do not to knock, or even just enter on his own.

He eats quietly.

The palace staff have taken his measurements and his opinion on color and style. He'll be fitted tomorrow for the ball in three days time.

He sighs, running a hand through his hair, mussing the curls. There's a large, clawed foot tub he's been eyeing, but he needs to do something first.

He knocks on the door, praying that is the only thing separating them.

"Come in." Her voice muffled.

Percy pushes on the unlocked door, a flurry of silks and tule and lace greeting him. Alyce stands on a dais, maids pushing their way around her with different fabrics and jewels.

"Should I come back later?"

"Stay." She meets his eyes over a fall of plum lace, her face bright. "Help me choose a color, the style is already spoken for." She tries to keep a straight face as pins push and swirl pale fabric into place over her body, the plain foundations for beauty.

"I'm not sure I'll be helpful." He steps cautiously into the room, ducking as a man bears bolts of velvet and cashmere on his shoulder.

"What color are you wearing?" She calls through the cream chamise being pulled over her head.

"I can't tell you, it's a surprise."

Alyce pouts through the lace blocking her view.

"I think your dressing was easier than mine. This isn't even the fitting yet."

Percy chuckles. "Do you need a break?"

"No. Just finish quickly please, I don't know how much longer I can stand here." A maid nods at her request.

"Plum." Percy says, eyeing the silk next to her dark skin tone.

"Plum?" Alyce arches a brow.

"Yeah, plum." Percy shoves hands into his pockets. "Makes your eyes glow. Like the moon."

"Plum it is."

Alyce plops down on the bed as the last of the maids leave, a flurry of strings and fallen pins in their wake. She releases a groan.

"This is why I dislike the royal court."

"Being waited on hand and foot?" Percy jokes.

"No," she twists, eyes gazing up at him. "Being told what to do. Who to be. Clothing worn for status and rank and not personal taste. I dislike the whole show of it all. It never feels real. Until it is."

Percy crosses his arms, leans against her bedpost.

"When is it real? When you receive secret notes from Princes, or when you claim to run from a hospital to get away from your father, only to walk into the high court knowing he is likely to be here?"

Alyce squeezes her eyes shut, turning her face from him. "Percy, please."

Percy takes two steps, bending to the floor beside her bed because his legs may give out, takes her hand.

"Who are you, Alyce Chime? I'm not stupid, do not lie to me."

She's not looking at him. His brave, kind, passionate love is refusing to meet his gaze. Worse still, she's afraid.

She heaves in a wobbling breath. "When I told you I ran from my father, that was the truth. So was leaving my home unknowing to him. I've meant every word I've ever said to you. Every moment has been honest."

"So, what hasn't been honest? What have you kept from me, because as far as I know, Princes do not give notes to girls they don't know."

"Well," she shrugs, eyes going cat like. "They might." She licks her bottom lip.

Percy swats her knee. "Not like that!" But he is smiling too. He sighs, laying his head on her knees. "I love you, Alyce, from the first letter you sent me.

If something is happening in your life, I want to know. I want to support you, in all you do."

She bites the inside of her cheeks, holding back tears.

"Oh, Percy." Wet splashes fall onto his cheeks.

He crawls on the bed beside her, holds her close to his soul. Their bodies curling together, her heart beat too fast to be honest. Percy doesn't mention it. He whispers against her neck, leaving kisses, soft as butterfly wings. She sighs, pressing impossibly deeper.

They don't speak, though questions still burn between them. Foolish as it may seem, Percy is afraid of her answers. Afraid of weighted words between them. He has seen so much of her soul, that he doesn't care how her mind or body take form.

Forever he would wait, formless and star filled if it meant their souls were always intwined.

But souls are honest with each other.

The moon has risen, casting silver light through glass windows. Alyce asleep in his arms. Percy moves slowly. Untangling legs and de-clasping arms, he slips off the edge of the bed. He brings blankets up to her chin, leaving a butterfly kiss on her forehead. Alyce shifts, Percy holds his breath. She doesn't wake.

It's wrong, he knows. If trust is built on steady ocean waves, his is rain, coming in spurts and little down pours. Alyce could have hidden the paper from him, she didn't have to take his hand, didn't need to let him know something had transpired he was too careless to see. He should trust her to tell him in time. Still, he doesn't stop as he carefully rummages through her bag, searching between the pages of books and the inside pockets of coats.

His fingers finally close around curled paper, buried deep in the fabric of a skirt, a small, quickly drawn map. Seems too old, refolded too many times to be the paper from the prince.

He keeps searching. The clothes she wore are empty and the books she carried nothing but poetry and odd quotes.

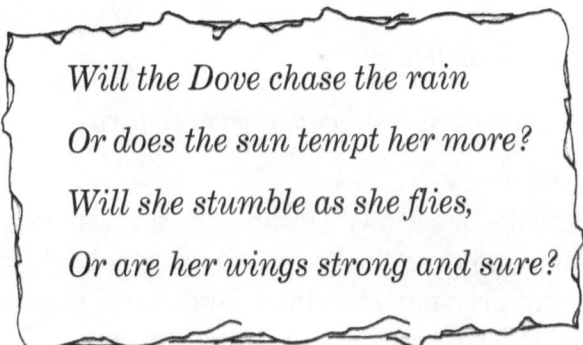

Will the Dove chase the rain

Or does the sun tempt her more?

Will she stumble as she flies,

Or are her wings strong and sure?

Percy closes the door between them with a click.

He sheds his clothes, turns out the light, and crawls into bed. He dreams of secret whispers and hidden passages and a King with red eyes, fire in his hands, burning his brother before his eyes.

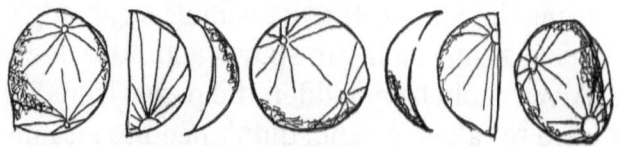

xix.

Alyce wakes when Percy pulls his fingers from hers. She waits while he rummages through her things, causing a ruckus and taking an excruciatingly long time. She almost sighs. He'd make a terrible spy. The thought makes her smile.

Finally, the door closes and she turns from the wall. Percy is gone. A few moments later, his light goes out and Alyce lies awake in the dark.

She hasn't read Rae's note yet, tucked to her chest. Couldn't bring herself to open it, to further betray Percy's beautiful trust.

She pulls it from her shift.

Second courtyard. Nine twenty-five. Guard rotation.

Alyce bites down a scowl. Despite her gut telling her to wait, to sleep and even to slip into Percy's bed if it will keep her from arriving, she stands and starts to dress. She almost doesn't make it, relishes the thought of wandering, getting lost, but her feet know the way as if they have walked them a hundred times.

Wearing her army jacket and slightly restricting pants, she pulls on the glass garden doors. The maze of roses and thick walls of jasmine intending to lose her amid flowers and fountains do not slow her; she knows the way.

She can see his frequency like a trail, a pathway guiding her to him. He must have walked the same corridors before Alyce slipped from her rooms.

She pauses by a low fountain, a dark figure with his back turned toward her. Boughless and taller than Prince Rae, she knows who she is meeting.

"Hello, father."

Jaal turns to her, skin silver in the light, bright as stars. He nods to her.

"Take a seat."

"I'll stand." Even now, after all this time, she feels her body go rigid. Her spine straightens, arms lock behind her, feet shoulder width apart. Boots polished to perfection, oh how clean she has kept them.

"I saw you arrived with someone." His voice trying for friendship.

"I didn't realize you cared. I've been missing for months." Hers is getting straight to the point.

"You've been on a mission for months. I assumed you needed a cover."

She growls. "What do you want?"

Even after all this time apart, her father is cold. He's never cared. She thinks. He still doesn't. There is something he wants.

"I come in Rae's stead. He requested this. Have you had any contact from King Silver?"

Her arms cross. "No, sir."

"Were you present when his highness and Lady Iliana first made contact outside of the marriage alliance?"

"No, sir."

"Yet you were with her Ladyship at this time, she told you nothing?"

"Iliana and I had been growing apart, she spoke less to me of her plans."

"You are her guard!" Jaal snaps, breaking his composure. "You left her in an enemy battlefield with no way home and no protection!"

"I was relieved of duty, I tried to follow her but was wounded in the attack." She tries to stay calm, tries to hone in her emotions but they crack through her like lightning.

Her father takes a step back; Alyce tries to remember the last time he saw her cry.
She lets her tears fall, a sudden overflow from years of suppression. Let him see.

She raises her head.

Jaal sniffs, uncomfortable for only a moment. "Lady Iliana is on her way here as we speak. She will come with liquid Glos, intended for King Usis."

Alyce's head spins.

"You will meet her on the eve of the ball, retrieve the Glos, and inject it into the King."

Alyce's heart stops beating. "You mean to-"

"King Usis is a terror to our country, to Ulna, and his own family. *King Silver* is giving her full support and Prince Rae has placed the steps in motion. I should not have to gain your support. You are not under your own rule, you belong to the throne of the Radian King, and this is now your mission."

"We've kept enough of King Silver's secrets. I won't kill him."

"If not you, my capable soldier, then King Silver herself will take matters into her hands, on order of Radian law. Tell me," he takes a step forward. Alyce frozen in place. "Will you let your charge place herself in harm's way, because that would be treason to the crown." Their eyes lock, fierce with unsaid words.

She doesn't respond.

Her father steps past her. "I trust you enough to know your answer."

Jaal leaves her, footsteps fade and Alyce loses control of her legs. She crumples to the ground of the garden floor, body numb, mind running.

She folds herself into prayer and doesn't rise until dawn touches her shoulders.

Rae finds her in the gardens, his steps languid and silent. She doesn't move from her vigil, legs long since lost connection to her brain. She cannot even feel them beneath her.

She raises her head as Rae sits on the fountain edge, legs crossed, mask silver, threaded with gold. She nods once to the Prince. The future King.

"Why have you brought Percy here? You could have sent for me alone, if it's true you knew where I've been all along."

"You cannot hide from the eyes of the crown, pretty bird." His teasing voice turns solemn. "My father sent for Waiden, I had Iliana's good word you would follow if you truly cared for him. She placed the message in the paper just in case."

Alyce laughs. "Here I've been, thinking I could build a life for myself, and you've had me as a puppet since the beginning." Her tone sour. She rises.

"Not every moment, love." Rae grins.

Alyce could hit him. Hard.

"Stop playing games with me. I will not be your weapon. I refuse."

"Then dainty Iliana will be left alone-"

"Do not use her against me! Iliana left me on the battlefield! I was too wounded to chase her, *again*, and after everything she has done-" Alyce throws up her arms. "I didn't give a care to *what might happen*. She's a capable girl. She'll figure it out."

No way on earth would she be able to speak to royalty like this, or anyone for that matter. But for two minutes, Alyce doesn't care- and she feels horrible about it. She wants to care. Wants to be the kind, loving, determined girl buried in her soul, but come circumstances, she has to keep her buried. Because the girl inside her is too kind, has too much faith, and doesn't believe in war.

This anger is the fire she uses to keep herself safe, only she doesn't want to burn any longer.

Doesn't want others to have the capability to throw coals on her fire and watch her rise again, this time for their bidding. This fire only burns others, as much as it eats away at her.

"Let me go, Rae. I don't want this anymore."

Rae stands, slender, taller than Percy with his towering boughs, today painted white with black ash eyes. His gloved hand cups her cheek, runs a thumb over her zygomatic bone.

He leans down, as if to kiss her, hiding his words from watching eyes.

"Do this for me, for yourself- and I will ensure you live a long and uneventful life. Your past wiped clean if that's what you wish, free to be with your healer boy with no fuss about past sins."

"The only past sin I would have will belong to you." She hisses the words, tilting her head into his neck. An embrace of poison.

"Ah, little dove, how perfect you are." He kisses each of her cheeks; Alyce's fists curl.

"I will see you at the ball, it's sure to be a smashing party." He pulls away, leaving her too hot, burning with rage inside.

Grabbing her boots, she allows her mind to burn once more with fire. Protecting thoughts she keeps only to herself. Brown eyes. Scarred hands. Words written on paper. Words that have given her wings.

She will protect them all, even if she must burn the world down to do it.

PRINCE

OF

FLOWERS

Sharp memories invade Rae's mind. He
is eleven.

Usis beckons Onol forward, she walks as if
pushed by a poker, every step agony, toward their
father.

Rae watches, still young, skin unmarred. So
naive. Usis loved them, even as he forced Rae to
watch while he beat his sister.

Usis loved them. They needed their kingdom to
be strong, they needed Usis to be strong- to protect
them. So Rae held out a trembling hand, to see how
much force it would take Usis to burn him.
His father didn't flinch at his screams.

He is fifteen.

Onol joins the Faith of the Divine Hum, living in
the palace Temple, leaving Rae alone.

Usis has developed electric sunlamps, ones based
on his own power. He has sat in a locked room for
days, burns blooming along his skin, his father's
angry energy pulsing from the machine.

Sixteen.

Rae defies his father going to war, earning a ruined
face and a new name. The Flower Prince, for the
blooms he uses to cover his face, a declaration to
his people he is not a monster of light like his
father, but a man of earthy growth. The masks
come later, when he doesn't have the strength to
grow new petals each day. Now, he barely feels the
power in his veins, the life under his skin. He is
only a shadow, a puppet for the King. The war rages
and Usis only grows stronger.

Eighteen.

Rae engaged, to a woman he doesn't know the face
of, bearing an unfamiliar voice. Until the letters start.
Until they talk for months and then meet in Kilo,
briefly and only once. Until they strike a plan.

Rae fingers her latest letter. The paper worn from
folding and refolding and his bare fingers tracing
the words.

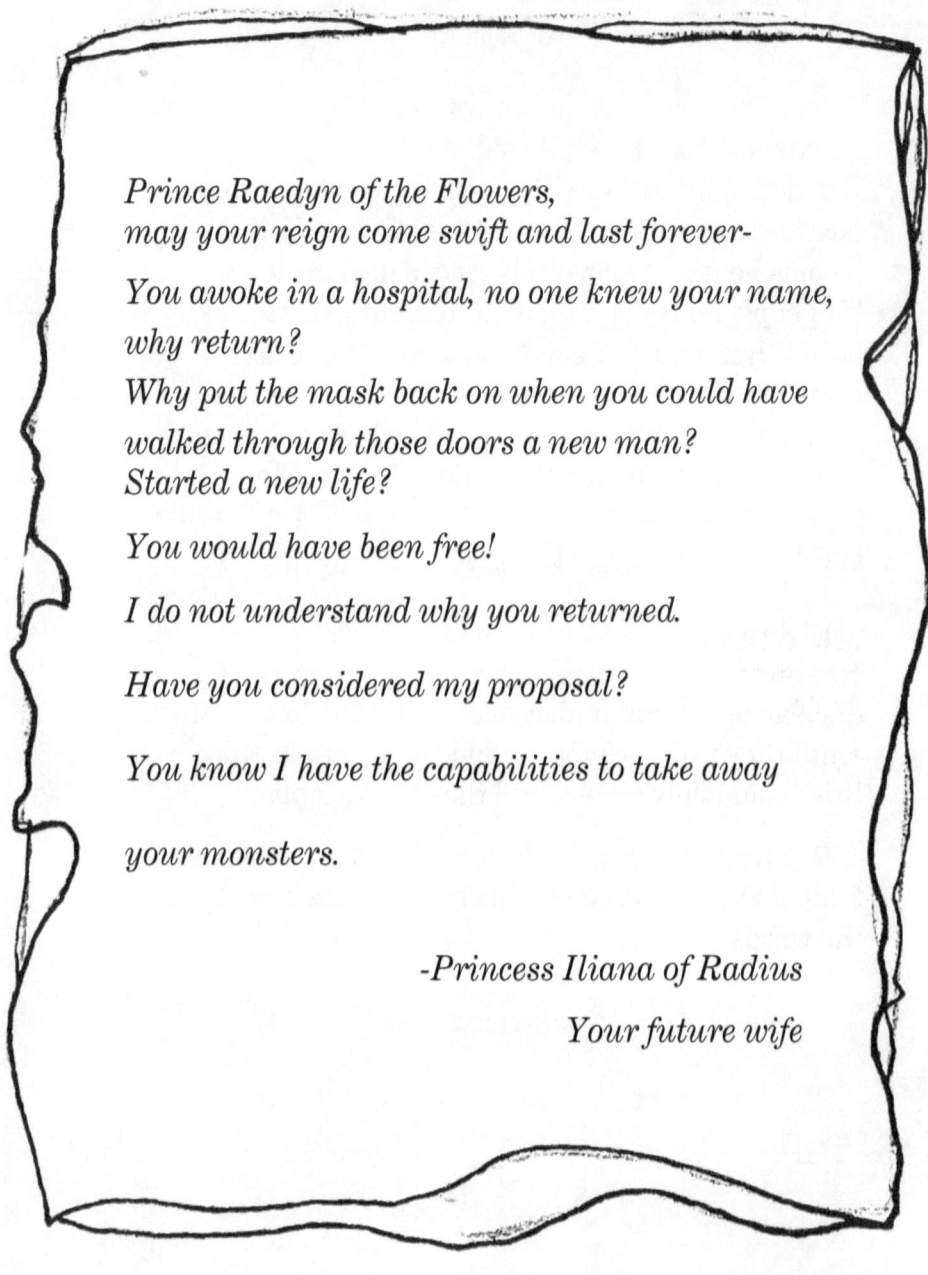

Prince Raedyn of the Flowers,
may your reign come swift and last forever-

You awoke in a hospital, no one knew your name,
why return?
Why put the mask back on when you could have
walked through those doors a new man?
Started a new life?

You would have been free!

I do not understand why you returned.

Have you considered my proposal?

You know I have the capabilities to take away

your monsters.

-Princess Iliana of Radius

Your future wife

Rae remembers his reply, keeps the words in his
head to imagine her reading them. Over and over.

Princess Iliana of Radius, may your rule be mighty and memorable-

Even before the war, father spoke of an alliance with Radius through marriage. A peace treaty Usis was giddy to make.

Father has been crazed to get his hands on an Alom; I was afraid he would continue his experiments on you. The papers were already signed, our fates sealed.

I knew as far as I ran, there would always be that girl I left to his mercy. I wouldn't do that to you, even though we had never met.

Iliana, will you do something for me?

Something that will allow us to make our own choices in life, as long as we live- separate or together.

Crown Prince Raedyn,

Expectantly awaiting your return

Rae clicks his drawer open, drops her letter inside. Locks it again. Drops the key in his glove pocket.

He is a man of locked drawers and secrets and treason in his heart. Treason, or loyalty to his people?

Rae draws a shaking hand over his scarred face. "Iliana, where are you?"

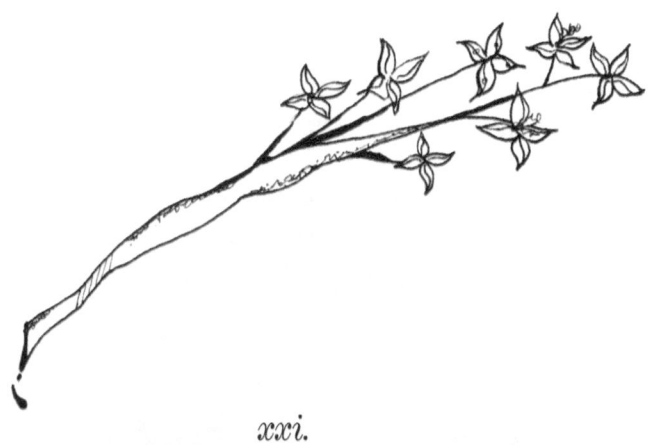

xxi.

Percy is dressed in red. Crimson as the dawn and the royal seal tamped onto letters and invitations. He pulls his collar with an ivory gloved hand, sleeked curls touching the nape of his neck. Gold buttons and gold embroidery. A belt at his waist, ivory pants, dark, glossy shoes.

There is a soldier in the mirror. The shadows darkening his hair and suddenly he is Ojo. He touches his hand to the glass.

"You have to let me go, Ojo. I need to live now." The image doesn't speak. His brother doesn't speak. Percy pulls away.

A hopeful knock draws him to Alyce's door on instinct, but it is the main door which opens, Frederik waiting in royal finery.

"I shall escort you to the ball, Mr. Waiden."

"Let me see if my date is ready-"

"Unnecessary. Miss Chime shall join you later, the King wishes you to have your own entrance."

"I understand. One moment please." Percy politely shuts the door on the man's baffled face. He knocks on the only door that matters. This, and maybe the exit.

"Alyce?"

No answer. No sound to let him know she is near. They've barely spoken in the past two days. Alyce woke before him the night of his treachery, watched him with knowing eyes. He was ready to apologize, ready to confess, when Alyce slipped into her rooms with a distant gaze and hasn't removed herself since.

After reassuring maids said that she wasn't ill, wasn't crying, wasn't missing, wasn't visiting the Prince- Percy gathered she needed time. He slipped letters under her door, yet never received any in return. This door has been locked. He doesn't try the handle.

"I'm being taken in early. I mean to steal a dance with you, if you'll have me, so I better see you there." He laughs, but it does not close the distance between them.

"Alyce, I love you. If there is something going on, truly, I want to be here for you. Will you let me in?"

A letter slips under the door. A sketch. Nadala standing on the moon, reaching for Lor's letters.

Percy folds the paper, slipping it into his jacket.

"I will wait for you, Nadala. Forever and a day. I will continue to wait."

He pulls from the door, the gate between their souls, allows Frederik to draw him away. It feels as if he has left his heart in that room.

Then the door opens, plum skirts and blue pearls greet him. There is Alyce, hair trimmed short and curled atop her head, boots gleaming on her feet, a little unusual for a ball, but Percy doesn't care.

She smiles, hesitant and slow, her face painted with glittering silver, casting her in starlight.

Percy extends a hand she places a chill gathering of fingers into. Skin soft, hands for mixing Afiya and gathering flowers and writing letters to strangers. Hands that hold only gentleness.

"Forever, Percy?" She arches a brow. "It seemed to me you were leaving."

"Only to gather more ink." He kisses her hand. "Write you enough letters to build a bridge with."

"I think we already have." She laughs, though it is strained.

"No, not yet. It will take a lifetime of letters. A lifetime I am willing to wait for."

She stills. "But if I reveal all my thoughts to you, all my secret wishes, and past lives, would you still wait?"

"If there is a storm brewing inside you, I will weather it by your side."

Alyce blinks. "I'm going to ruin my makeup."

"You'll also be late for your announcement if you don't hurry." Frederik adds, steps mannered and quick.

Percy tugs her along, gently, and with a smile, his heart easing at the sight of her.

They reach the ballroom without fanfare, fingers hot between them.

Frederik leaves them with a flourish in the hall and for a moment, they stand before wide double doors, thrown open into the light of the Sun King's court.

"Ready?" Percy turns, eyes drifting to hers.

Alyce slips in a shuddering breath, face pale as dark starlight. Then her eyes harden, tough as diamonds and fierce as winter storms. She takes his arm, fingers on his crimson sleeve. Silver eyes on his.

"Percy. My time with you has been, for the first time in my life, something I've done for me. Against the rules and orders of my father and even Radian law, I choose you. If I had to relive every moment of my trapped life, I would, because they led me to you. And see," she smiles, raising a hand to his cheek. "Even in this worldly disobedience, the Divine Hum reigns."

"What are you telling me, Alyce?" He tries to keep the fear from his voice, yet it slips from his eyes. From his heart, jumping in his chest.

"We don't know what will happen tonight. Loyalties shift."

"Mine don't. Mine will never shift."

Her eyes sadden. "Who are you loyal to?"

"The Divine. My brother. King Usis, even if he is a beast, he is still the anointed sovereign. You. Alyce," he takes both of her hands in his. "What has you so afraid? You're trembling."

She pulls her hands from his. "I fear only the future, only the unseen."

"Then let me open your eyes, let me show you the unseen."

Percy takes her delicate face in his hands, kisses her slowly, gently. "Stay with me, Alyce Chime. Always." He touches his forehead to hers.

"I will. Always." She sighs, sharing his breath.

They walk into the light, unafraid of being blinded.

xxii.

"I noticed your bride seems to be missing." Usis shifts in his throne. Rae remains perfectly still.

"She *is* coming, father."

Usis sniffs.

The dancers and nobles drip down the grand stairs, dressed in golds and blues and shimmering greys. The red of a jacket catches his eyes. Percy is among the crowd, an angel in dark plum on his arm.

They make a fine pair, Rae sips from his fermented Afiya. The healer and the soldier. The healer who was a soldier. The soldier who is a healer, if she knows it or not. Rae sinks into his chair, legs crossed. Black boots gleam at him, his grey coat ending in sharp points, the doublet smokey, hiding his scars. And, of course, his mask. His boughs are painted sharp green, stark against his dark attire, thick gold bands wrapping their twists and sharp turns.

His single glove tightens, stretched against his fist, his other hand ringed and hot to the touch.

Rae fears he will burn sitting here, next to the man who turns his own kingdom into ashes for forced alliances. Rae knows what his father wants, the power of the Alom.

A power he intends to give him, just not in the way his father wanted.

"I see the nurse who found you is here." Usis' voice is quiet amid the glittering ocher ballroom and melodic stringed music. Rae knows the implantations of this tone.

"What of it?" His is harsh.

"Oh, I intend to honor him tonight. As a thank you."

"For reuniting you with your beloved son?"

"For saving a worthless boy, who will only bring Ulna to ruin."

"A fine thing for you I am moving to Radius." Another sip. *Yes, let him pay for what he has done.* A dark voice hisses in his mind.

Usis slips cold eyes to him. Eyes that radiate heat the next moment. "Your place is here."

"Yet you don't want me." Rae leans into the thing inside him, feeling power. "You'd prefer I became amiable like my sister and bowed to your will. You don't want a challenger living in your house."

"Is this a threat, Raedyn?"

Yes.

Rae stands, adjusting his coat. "Better be careful, Usis. There are a lot of eyes here tonight." He steps down the dais, his father's glare following him.

The crowd mills around their Prince, a tide shifting as he walks, drawing near yet never close enough to touch him. Never enough to be anything other than the recoil of his presence.
Rae has an impenetrable field of energy.
Until Flyn loops an arm over his shoulder, and they appear more as mischievous boys than young nobles of weight and power. Rae grins.

"Any pretty girls you'll be dancing with tonight?" Flyn chugs what is likely not his first drink, cheeks flushed.

"I think there is only one whose presence on my arm won't start a war..." A flash of deep purple, shimmering pearls and dark skin catch his vision.

Alyce stands at Percy's arm amid a group of healers from Halo Hospital. Usis wanted to *thank them*. Rae knows what those words mean.

"Excuse me a moment." He disappears from Flyn, drifting through the crowds a ghost. Alyce shifts as he enters the group.

"So, I have all of you to thank for my rescue."

"We were only doing our job, your highness." An emerald Etz, Rossi, bows deeply, a vest clinging to her torso and wide legged pants drape pointed shoes.

"No thanks are necessary, Prince." Percy presses a hand to his chest, the other lightly on Alyce's shoulder. She doesn't look at him.

"You keep saying that, Waiden, yet this is the only reason you are here." Rae spreads his arms to the grand, gold edged room, the dancers, the King on *his* throne.

"When the Sun King wishes to grant thanks, your decision doesn't matter anymore." His voice is a blade and Alyce jumps at its touch.

For a royal Alom guard, she scares too easily. Prays too often, perhaps. Afterall, the Divine never saved him. Why would she, or anyone, be the exception.

"A turn around the room, Miss Chime?" He extends an arm to her, one she takes after casting moon colored eyes to Waiden.

Rae reaches out, grips her hand. "One dance, I promise, then you will be free." He pulls her into position for a waltz, he didn't need one of the twisting line dances to interrupt him. He snaps, and the lights dim, the music slows.

She sways in his arms.

"Ready, little dove?"

She spins away from him, falling back into his grip with more force than necessary.

"I am not the dove in this story." Her voice iron.

"Yet you are not the sun, and now you are too close to its light. Only I can save you from burning." His grip tightens on her waist.

"I cannot do this, Rae." She whispers in his ear.

"You must." He hisses back, his breath a kiss unwanted. "Iliana is fragile. I am untrusted. Your father bears too many scars from the Diamond Wars; he is brittle and slow. You are petite. You are unknown. You are-"

"I am not even full diamond. Do you know what that means?" She stops, skirts and polished boots spin around them, a river purling around a stone. "I am breakable, Rae. Not indestructible."

Rae pulls her in on a high violin note, strings singing. "Then you must be careful. It is you, or King Silver herself."

Alyce shoves away from him. "Let the King come, it is time she took a stand in her own wars."
She slips through the crowd of yellow and ocher and red as a bruise. A wine stain on his plans.
Rae clenches his hands.

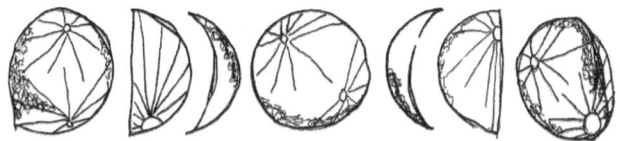

xxiii.

"You're trembling."

"I'm fine." She doesn't mean to snap, holding onto his arms like a lifeline. Alyce's vision slips between black and Percy's worried features.

"You need to sit down. I'll get you a drink." He's taken on his nursing voice, commanding yet gentle. She does as he bids.

A familiar nurse with frosty green boughs fans her with his orchestra pamphlet. She is glad Jasmine is nowhere to be seen. She couldn't deal with another mess tonight.

"Here." Percy hands her a pale moon Afiya, and Alyce drinks it as if it is the cure to all that ails her. Pure moonlight, sliding down her throat, guarding her from shadows. She can only hope this will truly protect her, that she might be spared from becoming a monster.

She squeezes her eyes shut, blocking out Percy's face.

This is not the time for a panic attack, she scolds herself. She is a soldier, and she needs to *act like one.* Yet she is acting like one. Her duty to her father, and her kingdom kept her from Percy these past two days. If she had seen his face, answered

226

even one of his careful letters, her earthly loyalty would have shattered, shoved from her soul like acid.

It was the soldier in her who kept her planted on her feet, firm in these twisting tides of war and uncertainty. Usis may be a monster, but if she follows Rae's plan, then so is she.

Perhaps it is better this way. Even if she hadn't been ordered as Iliana's guard, the Divine asked her to remain by the Princess's side. Just once more she would follow a path she has no desire to walk.

Then she will be free.

Please, my Divine One, let me stay with Percy. Let me live a life of sundresses and market days and starry nights. There are no stars in Radius. I didn't realize their effect on me.

I do not know if I could live without them.

My Divine, lead me in a path of gentleness. A life of peace and sunshine. Let me build a life here, with him, with the sun.

Divine Hum, bless Percy. Bless his health, his mind, his heart, his works, his actions, his dreams, his desires, his thoughts, his memories. Let him turn toward You for life, peace, joy, strength, work, desire. I ask You are his all and every.

Please, bless him. He needs You.

Darling Divine, here are my hands, I give them to You. Here are my feet, let them always lead me to You. I want my life in Your hands. I want Your Truth and values to be the pillars of my journey.

So many prayers she has prayed, begged, sung, spoken, cried.

Alyce looks down at her dress, a laugh escaping her lips. This is the first time she has worn a dress, a real one. Percy looks so perfect, staring down at her.

She stands, pretends the step she takes is one onto new ground. Passing the glass aside, she takes his hand.

"Dance with me." The words are roaring inside her, yet come out a plea.

Percy's grin creeps up his face, he pulls her closer and he is nothing like Prince Rae when he whispers in her ear.

"Stealing my words, love?" A kiss lands on her cheek. "Asking you is my job."

"I'm just being progressive."

He laughs, guiding her once more and as if for the first time, onto the dance floor, his face sunlight.

"At least you are smiling now."

"I wasn't before?"

Percy shakes his head, the hair gel overworking to keep each curl in place. "Not with him."

"Well, I've never danced with a Prince. I was nervous."

"And I've never wanted to hit someone before. First time for everything."

She whacks his shoulder, taking her position. A long line of dancers forming on either side.

"You'll get in trouble, talking like that. Treasonous."

"Maybe you are worth committing treason for." They take a step away from each other, men on one side, ladies across.

"I hope you mean that."

The music starts. They step forward, feet an inch apart, then hands meet, gentle, at the wrist. A kiss. The ladies look away, the men pull their chins with soft fingers.

They step back, feet swooping in an arch across the floor as they spin away, the drums start. A build in the music, a lone flute carrying the aching melody; a reunite of dancers. Careful eyes and cast glances across the mirrored floors. It's the kind of dance done on summer nights, with high stars and glowing smiles. An entwining dance of pulling and pushing, leaving and reuniting. A reminder that the other is never alone.

Alyce feels as if every life she has lived has been profound, a step guiding her to *this* life, this dance. Soft brushes between rows. Swooping arms and quick feet. Every breath searching, waiting for the one who reflects the air she gives.

She is Alom. Her body has been the foundation of seas. The peak of mountains. The dirt between flower roots. The space beneath trees.

Now she is here, and this is the only life that matters, because Percy could never have been in the others. She would have remembered.

They twist and turn, meet and twirl away. Eyes cast low, almost shy. This is a side they have never met. A side of each other they have been waiting to embrace.

Dancing does something to the soul. Wakes a fire for life long dormant. One taste is never enough. One step out of hundreds of thousands already perfect. Dance is an open communication with the Divine, and they spoke hand in hand to the radiant Hum.

"Alyce, I-"

The ballroom doors swing open, unbolted by Flyn, who studies the late arrival with a dangerous sort of rapture. He extends a quivering ringed hand to a girl atop the steps.

Iliana.

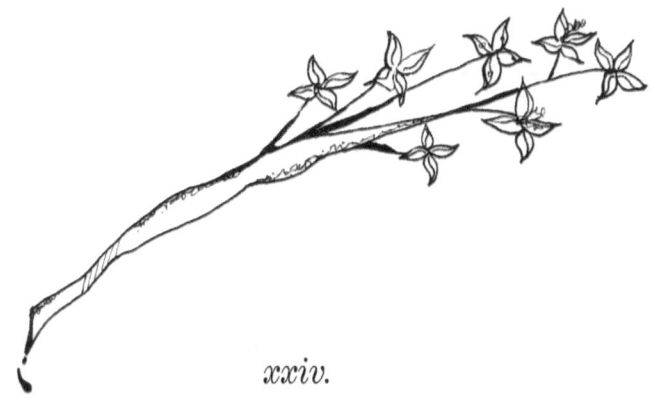

The woman atop the steps is stunning.
Hair coiled strands of emerald and verdant and greens.
Her Alom skin gleaming and rainbow hued,

made from abalone shell. Dress white, it trails
behind her as she descends, head raised. Pearls
dangle from ribbons and loop through her hair.

Alyce tenses in his arms. He pulls her a smidgen
closer.

Rae makes his way through the statue crowd,
frozen from her entrance. Frozen from the lock of
gazes across the dance floor. Rae has eyes only for
her.

The Prince bows to the Alom Princess, who waves
a fluttering hand. The music begins once more and
the two join the circle.

"Are you alright?" Percy pushes a drooping coil
from Alyce's forehead.

She nods distantly, finding his eyes once more. The
gold lights above turn her gaze into liquid metal.

"I am."

"Perhaps we should leave? I think we have both
had enough of this night."

232

"I- I want too. Percy, I want too." Her gaze trails back to the Princess, clutched in the Prince's arms. The music begins to die down, Alyce pulls him close. She presses a hot kiss to his lips, slipping past his barrier of teeth and false smiles. She soaks into him, infusing their souls with the frequency of love.
Of goodbye.

"Whatever happens- know I love you." She pulls away, leaving him cold.

"Alyce, wait!" But she has slipped from his arms, making her way through the crowd as if pulled by some invisible force.

She approaches the Princess, Iliana casting triumphant eyes to him, and Percy watches as they disappear down a spare hall together.

He blinks. His own vision a liar, it must be. It's true, though, what he sees. His love leaving him alone.

He hesitates, half a moment, then follows her through the crowd. Shoving dancers and nobles from his path, battling through silks and flashing gems.

"My citizens," King Usis stands from his throne, a Temple clothed woman beside him. "Please, join me in welcoming Princess Iliana from Radius." Thunderous applause. Percy stumbles, loosing sight of which direction Alyce took.

The King raises a hand. "And the thanks to the one who discovered my son." The King's hand extends to him.

Percy swallows.

Several clap him on the back, giving encouraging words he cannot comprehend as he is ushered unwillingly toward the throne. Frost follows, and Rossi is close behind.

King Usis waits on his throne. Tall, gold painted boughs reach up from his head, tips sharpened points. The Sun King is dressed in golds and ochers and light casts down from his gaze.

"May it be known Ulna is kind to the people who do it good." Usis says officially.

Rae rolls his eyes beside him, mask tight over his features. It must hurt, pressing on the scars like that.

Percy shakes the thought from his mind. He considers the Prince lucky not to have his fist in that pretty face.

King Usis snaps, and three gold chests are brought out, placed at their feet.

"A gift." The King smiles. A chill scampers over Percy's spine. "Now, I would speak with the one who first discovered Prince Raedyn."

Rae gives Percy an urgent glance, but doesn't move from his stance.

"Please, don't keep me waiting again." The King chuckles. Percy has to swallow his dread, acid sliding back down his throat. They should have left, even ten minutes before and Alyce wouldn't be gone and he would be able to see clearly. His vision flashing dark and light.

A guard ushers him to a separate room, King Usis taking a different route.

Percy stands alone in a dim hallway, opening to another dance room, the guard leaving him with only a curt nod.

He doesn't move. Doesn't step forward. Doesn't turn around. Despite his feelings, he remembers Rae's words their first day here.

Usis wanted war.

Usis bombed his own city.

Now he is alone with the feared Sun King.

There is movement across the hall, a shifting of shadows like an old song breaking into new light. Only there is no light to break into.

Until Usis arrives, his very presence a radiant torch in the mirror walled room, flashing a thousand jagged King's. The Prince at his side.

Percy pulls in a breath, ready to step forward, into the light of the Sun King, but he is frozen. For the shadow has stepped forward first from the other side of the room, and he recognizes those moon eyes.

Alyce.

Percy curses his stunned form. The shock keeping him in place.

Alyce steps before the King, head high. The seam line of her dress is cut, giving more mobility. Showing more of her dark skin.

"Yes?" Usis raises a brow, as if nothing is out of the ordinary.

"I am here to apologize." Alyce grips something in her fist, catching the light of the King, flashing like a fallen star between her fingers.

A needle.

Percy takes a step forward. King Usis is laughing, turning away from her as he wipes his eyes.

Alyce shoots Percy a glance, panic overtaking her features at his presence. She shakes her head ever so slightly, warning him back.

"You?" Usis takes a step closer; Percy's stomach clenches. Rae does nothing, a wicked expression coming over his face as Alyce lifts her chin. Rae mouths something to her. Alyce doesn't flinch.

There are only feet between her and the King.
Only feet between love and obsession.

Alyce casts Percy one quick glance, her words to the
King slow. "I wish to apologize for my people.
For what we are about to do." She darts forward, the
needle gleaming in her hand like the fangs of a snake.

Usis takes a step back, stunned. Alyce jumps,
aiming for the throat, a dark syringe locked in her
grip.

Percy is moving forward, running, as the King's
eyes start to glow.

"Apologize?" The King roars, grabbing Alyce by
the throat mid leap. She gurgles, kicking at his
sternum, the syringe falling from her hand.

Before Percy can blink, light pours from the
King's hand and he throws her across the room.
Alyce lands with a thud against the pillars, rolling
just in time as another bolt escapes Usis's grip,
striking the ground beside her. Mirrors shatter, the
curtains ignite with flames.

The King walks forward, slow hunter and
wounded prey. Heat builds in the room and Percy
blinks panic from his gaze, pushing away old
memories.

I will not burn.

I will not lose her to fire!

The words scream in his head.

Rae has fear painted on his face, rich and red as the King's eyes.

Alyce is on her feet; Percy grabs the syringe from the ground, scraping the tiles. Angry liquid swirls in his grip, a storm inside the glass. The King swings, fire in his grip, reflected in his eyes. Alyce dodges and Percy is *so close*. Another foot…

"Percy, no!" Alyce reaches out for him, distracted. The King's wicked light shatters over her face. Alyce's scream cuts short with a deafening *crack*.

Percy falls, skidding against the ground, and plunges the needle into the King's greater saphenous vein, the tip breaking off. The glass shatters as Percy shoves the poison into the King's ankle.

The King stills, body stiff as he turns to Percy, his jaw working. "What have you done?" The words jagged and pained. "What. Have. You. Done!" But then he is not looking at him, but at Raedyn.

Percy scrambles back on his hands and feet, Usis lifts curled hands, trying to gain mobility in his fingers. Fire sparks and flickers in his palms.

Percy pushes himself onto his feet, lands with a jolt on his knees next to Alyce. Gently, he takes her face in his hands, turns her toward him. A crack runs from her left cheek, over her nose and cuts down to her right jaw. Eyes opened, shocked. She cannot see him.

Percy pulls her closer.

The King is still screaming, crawling inch by inch toward his son, who wears a stupid, triumphant look. Usis's skin has gone grey, his joints immobile, yet still he fights the poison in his veins.

"Are you going to kill me father? I think it is too late."

Percy covers Alyce's face with his hand, shields her eyes as Usis gains one last millimeter of strength, pulling the glass from his ankle with a snarl, and throws it at his laughing son with all his might. Rae falls back from the force of flames and sharp glass, clutching his chest.

"If I go... you burn with me." Usis breathes his last words, the grey reaching his mouth, his eyes. It crawls up his boughs and down his hands and then he is still. Statute. Stone.

The fire extinguishes. The lights disappear. Everything the Sun King has illuminated evaporates into air. Their city plunged into darkness.

Percy rocks Alyce back and forth, murmuring words he wishes he could remember now under his breath.

Rae staggers, curses, but Percy doesn't care. His trembling hands can only do so much, only help one at a time. Percy chooses to be selfish.

"Love? Can you hear me?"

Alyce hasn't moved. Hasn't blinked. Hasn't breathed. The gash is deep enough to slice through bone, yet she doesn't bleed, just stares at him with unseeing eyes.

Doors fly open and guards and maids and screaming officials flood the room.

The Princess is the first to their side, face oddly calm as she speaks, placing an even hand over Percy's trembling one. A spark slips through his skin, Alyce flinches in his arms.
Percy starts to protest, yet the Radius Princess interrupts him, voice cold. "She failed her mission."

Iliana meets Percy's eyes, as if waiting for him to comfort her too. "I ordered her to do this. She failed! Now she is no better than a traitor." A chill enters him at her words, snaking down his spine like ice.

Percy doesn't speak, doesn't know if he is able. Another crouches beside them while others examine the King and Prince. The man wears a placid expression, coat gleaming with the insignia of Radius. The same coat Alyce showed up on his doorstep wearing. The man is silver in the lack of light, though Percy knows how he must appear in the sun. Full color caught in his diamond skin.

Alyce's father.

The Princess kneels, furious beside them; silent tears stream down Jaal's face. "I can heal her. I can heal her, it's not too late."

"How?" Percy barks. "How will you fix this?!" His thumb is gentle over her broken cheek, yet trembles with rage all the same.

Jaal meets Percy's eyes with crystal clear ones, he examines the boy as one might a piece of parchment. Reading him on levels Percy doesn't wish to be read, yet bares his soul open.

"I thought you were part of her cover, a story to tell the crown, to slip into the King's court. Smart." Jaal looks at Percy's hands wrapped around his daughter. "Now I see that was a lie." Jaal holds out his hands. "My daughter. Time is of the essence, boy." His voice softens, ever so slightly. "I'll keep her safe. I promise."

Iliana's rainbow hues pale, Percy doubts it is with grief.

"Please, she must return to Radius before the crack sets too deep." Jaal implores.

"Then I will carry her." Percy stands, weightless and broken, Alyce limp in his arms. They hurry down halls and through doors. Panic echoes in every corner and shadows jeer at them.

They pass the ballroom and endless guest courters. Jaal stiff behind them and Iliana with a dry face and wary eyes.

They reach the courtyard. A hand clamps on Percy's shoulder, jolting him.

"Sir, the crown has requested you stay. You must remain in our custody until further notice." The guard is dead faced and expressionless, as if Kings turned to stone and wicked Princes are everyday life here.

"I need to get her to safety." He shrugs out of the guard's grip.

"Son, you should do what they say." Jaal gives the guards a pointed look.

"Don't call me that. You are no one's father if this is how you raise children." His grip on Alyce tightens, lifeless in his arms. Sightless. Voiceless.

"Two choices." Jaal states. "Waste more of Alyce's life arguing with me, and warrant yourself a blow, or remain here peacefully and hope the Prince knows what he is doing."

"You cannot ask me to choose that!"

"I just did, now what will it be?"

Percy eyes the guard, Jaal, the small, expressionless Princess at his side.

"Can you really save her?"

Jaal opens his arms. "There is only one way. She must become diamond. That, and only that, will give her new life. My daughter?"

Percy nods, numb. A hairline crack grows, edging toward her temple, as Jaal lifts his daughter.

The commotion sets in as Alyce is ushered away and Percy cannot find the strength to speak, too much noise invading his brain.

He has to follow her. Is all he can think as gravel
shifts underfoot, as he starts to run. He has to know she
will be okay.

Two guards wrestle him to the ground, gravel
sticking to his face, but Percy cannot see them.
There is only Alyce, draped in the arms of a man
she ran from. A man Percy has just handed her to.

Sol will know what to do. There is no need to
travel to Radius.

"Alyce! Alyce!" Percy starts to scream, the
armored gauntlets digging into his skin, slicing
new scars.

"I'm sorry- I'm so sorry." Emotion drains from his
body, down through his veins until he is empty. He
doesn't feel the guards lift him to his feet. Doesn't
see the blur of shadowed light and guests ushered
out. There is no light, not anymore.

There is nothing to see.

A

SEASON

PASSES

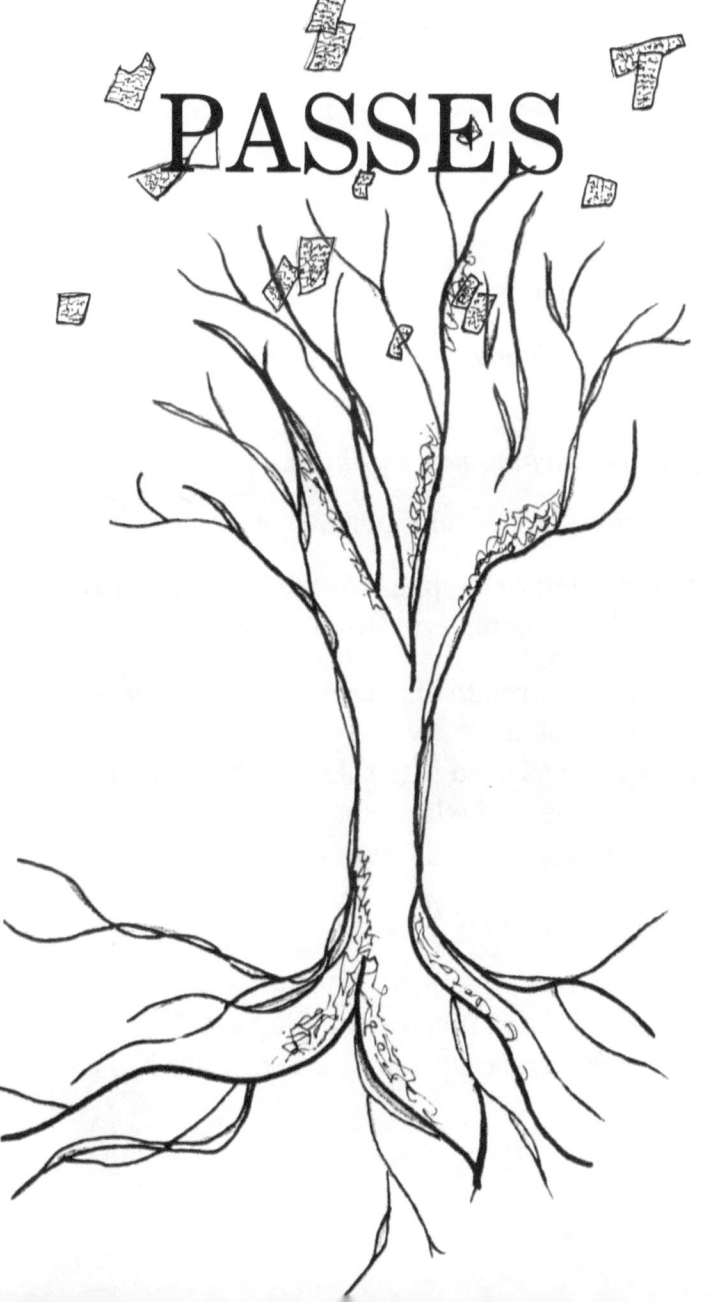

A weak King.

A cursed Prince.

Did you think you could escape us? We breathe with you.

There is nowhere you can hide...

The creature laughs in his head.

Raedyn curses, slumping down in the darkened hallway, clutching his eye. His chest.

Pain spikes through him, arching up his twisted boughs. Lives in his veins and arteries and joints. Everyday he has lived with this pain, the pain his father gave him in the last moments of his life, three months ago. Yet he rises still.

The people need their King.

The crowds cheer him on, his painted boughs red with orange licks of flame along the base. He dresses in red and crimson. Let them know he has survived his father. Let them know he has risen from the flames.

Unscathed.

A liar.

He stands atop the podium, sits in his father's throne, exhaustion weighting his bones. Onol is beside him, in the gowns of High Priestess of the Divine Hum. She will rule the Faith, while he rules the Kingdom.

Nobles and lords and officials and the rich from the city wait before him.

"Good people of Ulna," he stands, raising his arms. His hands quiver.

"Today we address the treason of Alyce Chime of Radius, who poisoned our great King. She is not here at this time, but it will be known throughout Ulna and Radius that Alyce Chime, along with the members of the Diamond Guard, are hereby banned from Ulna's shores forever from this day forth."

Painted faces and mournful eyes watch him, Onol silent behind him. Flyn's features are hard, hands rigid behind his back. Iliana waits beside him in dark hues. Her gemmed hand creeps up the ridge of his shoulder.

His headache worsens.

"Any contact with the Diamond Guard, any witness who does not report their whereabouts, is a crime of treason and punishable by the crown."

Yes...

"King Silver is devastated by the loss of her Guard, who have fled under Alyce's command. She is willing to work with us in their capture and return. I ask the same from Ulna. That is all."

He steps down, forcing slow breaths. Even as the crowd waits for him to leave, he is searching. For a pile of onyx locks. For eyes silver as the night sea. For skin the color of the sun.

Still, Alyce remains hidden from him.

She will be found. This thing with his father's voice hisses. ***She betrayed you. From the beginning Alyce has always been against you***- the name a curse, fearfully spoken.

"You are right." Rae whispers under his breath. "She betrayed me. She *left* me."

You never asked her to stay...

"Raedyn?" Onol places a hand on his shoulder, bringing his thoughts back to the light. Back to himself.

"Please see the order has been written. I- I need to rest."

"As you wish, brother." Onol bows, navy gowns pool at her feet.

Rae nods, the tremor piercing his soul, sending his head into splitting waves of worry and fear. Raedyn clamps shaking hands behind his back, exiting.

When he is alone he removes the mask. When he is alone, he drops the act. "Leave me alone!" He hisses. The dark thing hisses back, baring fangs.

I have work for you.

Alyce?

This isn't the first time I've written;

I know you are in Radius by now.

Your father rarely sends me updates, a few words,
but I treasure them.
Treasure knowing you are alive.

I've written to Sol, in case you were wondering, told
him I'm still in the palace- the King has yet to let
me leave.

He claims he needs a good healer by his
side; I've yet to see him.

I pray for you.

Everyday. Ask the Divine to guard
you, to bring you joy.
Oh, Alyce, I wish I could see you.

Your Love,
Percy Waiden

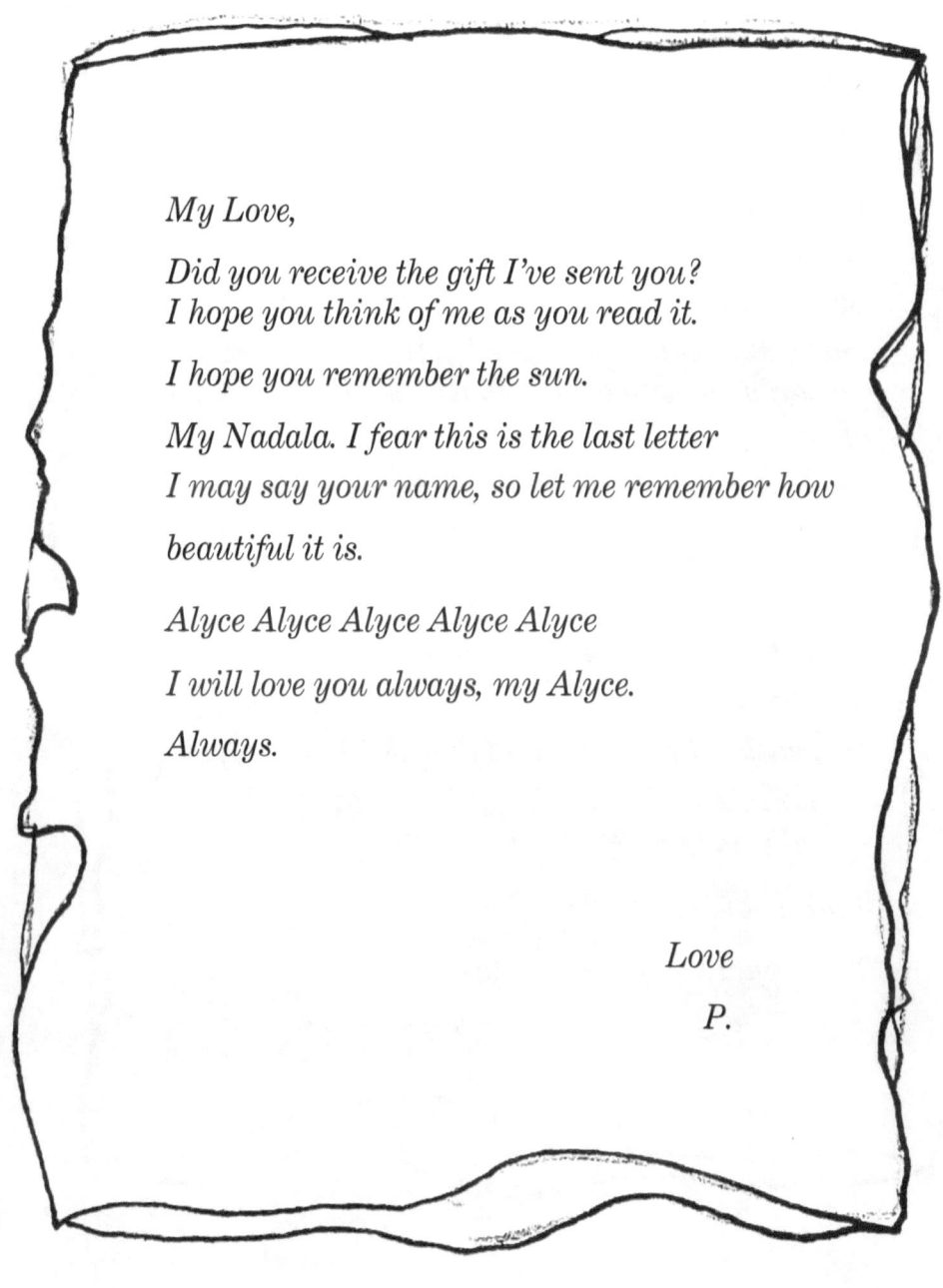

My Love,

Did you receive the gift I've sent you?
I hope you think of me as you read it.

I hope you remember the sun.

My Nadala. I fear this is the last letter
I may say your name, so let me remember how

beautiful it is.

Alyce Alyce Alyce Alyce Alyce

I will love you always, my Alyce.

Always.

Love

P.

My Nadala,

Still you have not written. Still I continue to pray.

I have never pleaded and asked and cried out to the Divine as I do now.

So many old wounds have been revealed to me. So many moments of hurt the Divine reaches out, touching me with gentle fingers, healing every part of me.

I will be a changed man when you return.

~~If you return.~~

I fear for the King. I never liked him before, yet now he is…different.

He spooks at hallways and dances from shadows. He mumbles when he thinks I cannot hear him. ~~He talks to himself.~~

I miss you, my Nadala.

You would know what to do.

With Love

Your Lor

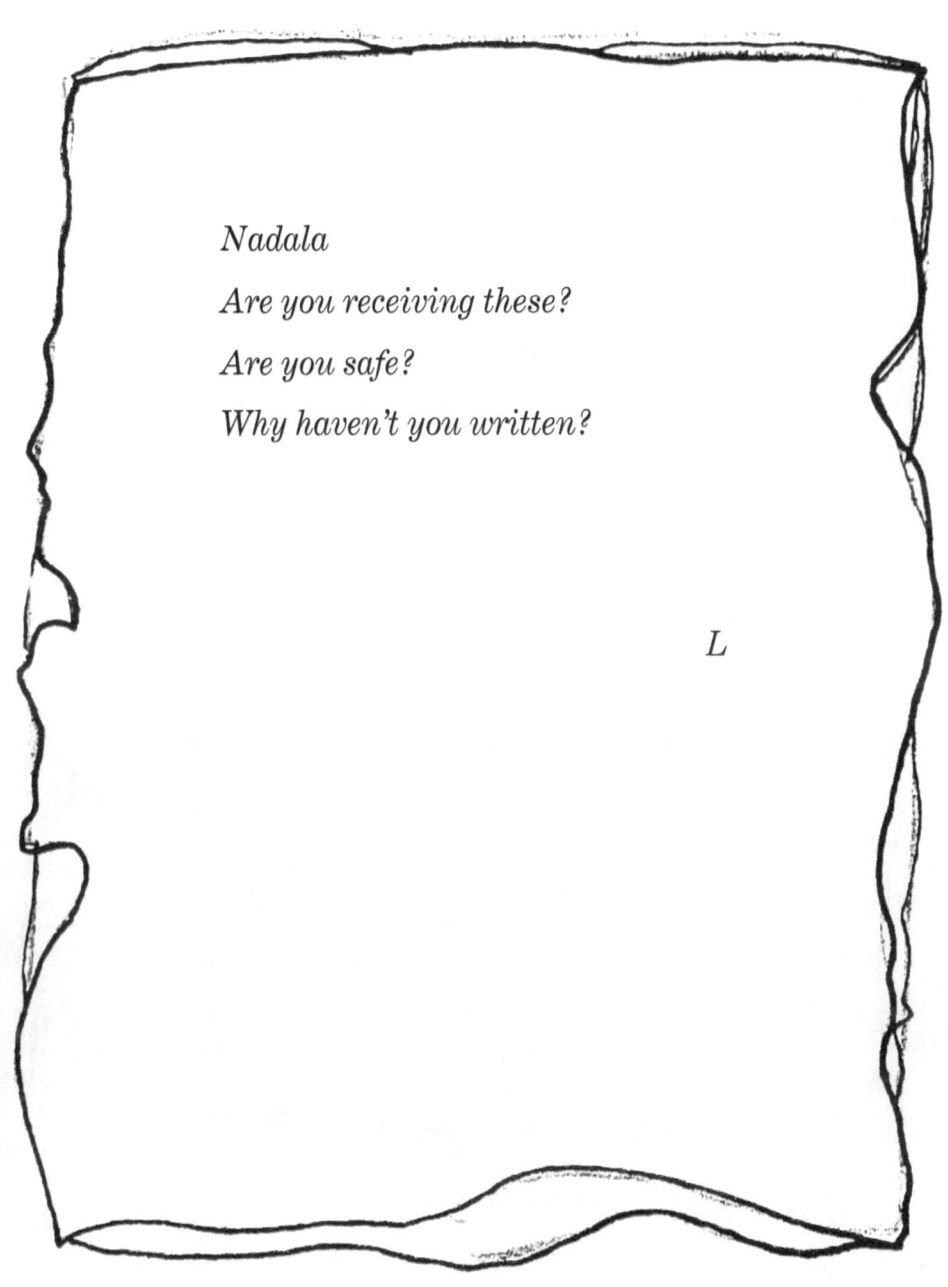

Nadala

Are you receiving these?

Are you safe?

Why haven't you written?

L

My Nadala

Turn your face to the sun.

Find some light while you sleep and heal.

Let my words ignite your soul,
bring you back to life.

Come, my love, write to me.

Tell me your troubles and fears and wants and
desires.

I will listen to every one.

I pour my heart to you, a barren ground.
Does love grow between us still?

Do you listen to my words, speak them aloud?

Can you hear me, my love?

I still wait for you.

Love

Lor

Nadala,

As flowers bloom only once,

I will love only once.

Only you.

*I know we haven't spoken, I know I'm doing this
without your consent, but I have placed a union
mark on my forehead, I have written vows intended
for only you to read.*

*I wait for you. I ask if you will have me as your
own.*

*I ask we work and build and grow alongside the
Divine together.*

You are light to me.

The sun in a land of darkness.

A guiding star.

You are also darkness.

*Reflection. The hands which
hold me, a guarding shadow.*

I know I have not received an answer yet.

I know I never may.

For now, I am yours.
I remain faithful to you,
Alyce Chime,
my Nadala.

I will wait forever.

Always Your Love

Lor

To Be CONTINUED

ACKNOWLEDGEMENTS

This story has been a joy to write!

I Am The Sun was born out of a dark winter when I desperately needed light and hope.

Percy and Alyce have certainly given that!

This has been a story of faith and courage and I pray it inspires you to always reach for the light of new growth.

These words came pouring from me, waking my creativity and passion for life.
My dear Hannah, this will always be for you, Nadala and Lor is your story and I thank you for sharing your heart with me. I love you.

Thank you to my family who circled wagons and helped me hit the ground running with the Destined Lore series. These books would not be the same without you!
My Divine Love, You know every need of our hearts. There are gentle souls and healing souls

and wounded souls who need reminders of Your Divine love and faith for them. May this be a love letter into the hearts of Your people. May this be an answer to someone's prayer. Remind us again of Your love.

Aryrejin El

March 30 2025

About the Author

Aryrejin El is the of author **WIND,**
Gentle Wild Things, and
I Am The Sun
She is a dancer, artist, entrepreneur and
teacher.
She has a great passion for life and
helping others fulfill their own lives and
live as they were meant to.
She writes words and stories of truth,
overcoming, and choosing life.
You can find her online at
www.Aryrejinel.com
On Instagram, or in the woods
somewhere.
Until the Next Tale!

I

AM

THE

STORM

Destined Lore II

Aryrejin El

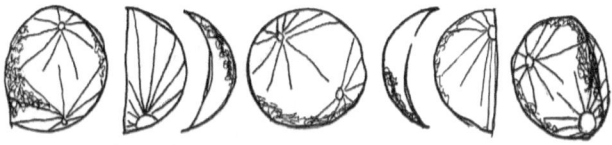

i.

She is a ghost.

Her breath empty, body numb.

She has not seen the sun. Doesn't remember the light. There are only pinpricks of shadowed luminance in her mind, faraway stars and lost memories.

She is a star herself now, one who has no light to shine. No faith to give. No love to receive. Perhaps she is not a star.

She remembers Iliana abandoning her. Remembers the destruction of Kilo. Remembers waking in an enemy hospital, terrified and alone, and the rest...

Blurry faces and lost names. Her father has told her little of her time away. Of the new scar along the bridge of her nose and the arch of her cheeks. A hazy milky way cutting across her crystal clear skin.

She drops the parchment, her grip rumpling its edges, words sliced under sharp fingernails. Every edge of her is a blade. A jagged piece.

She is not yet whole. Not yet ready to return... to whatever there was to return to. Perhaps nothing.

Perhaps she will never be able; her transformation has taken too long. Slowly, her body inches toward an existence as Yahalom, fighting with her previous self of condensed ions, minerals and soft stone. She has lost the little growth her body was able to produce.

Her prayers are hollow shells of themselves. Her faith used to sustain her, now she cannot lift a note of sound. She has not lost her voice, just the will to speak.

She is the strongest she has ever been; she has lost all strength.

"Will every new story I enter begin with the mourning of the one before it? My Divine, if this is what you have for me, then you must restore me. Build me up, for I am weary to even wake from sleepless dreams. We always talked, but now I cannot hear you."

"Perhaps you listen for a voice I do not have. Perhaps you truly do not want to hear My truth, fearful it will be different from your own."

She crumples on a ruined balcony, unafraid of the fall below her, overlooking the Silver King's domain. Mountains and deep seas and hidden places deep in the earth.

"Is Your truth different from mine?"

"I suppose that is up to you."

She sighs, pulling the bag from her shoulders, tugging the book from its depth. Fairy Tales. Hand painted. Original. The same one she held so long ago. She cannot remember the day she saw this book, cannot remember who she was with. A boy, she knows. She tears through its worn pages until she finds the story she seeks.

The Woman on the Moon.

Nadala.

Lor.

This story has been her only comfort. She doesn't remember why. Doesn't remember hearing it for the first time. Perhaps there was none. Perhaps she

has always known this tale, Jaal digging her from the ground with its truth woven into her tongue, painted across her mind.

She reads it for the hundredth time, searching for a way to her love from its pages.

Searching for a way home.

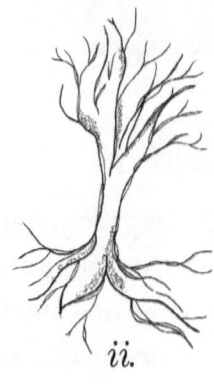

ii.

Candlelight wavers at her feet.

Prayers circling her breath. Knees numb from the stone floor.

Onol prays before the pulsing Ion Tree, light pumped from its roots. Through bough and branch it blooms and pushes, shoving its way to the surface, expressing itself in glowing leaves and soft blooms.

"Your light is beautiful, my Divine."

Onol waits, habitually, for a response. There is none. She holds in her sigh. The Divine will speak to her when her faith is enough. When her piety is sweet and her doubt small.

Perhaps she will wait forever.

"You continue to pray, my lady. You should be in the palace." A young Priestess, new to the faith, stands anxiously behind her.

Onol stands, expecting indents on the stones from her hours of prayer. There are none.

"I am High Priestess." She dips two fingers into pale paint, signifying her rank with the illuminance of the Ion Tree upon her dark forehead. "My place is here."

"The King has asked for you." The Priestess bows, nervous and fidgety, her blue gowns billow around her slim form, flowing sleeves drape the floor.

Onol swallows her spike of panic.

"I see." She folds her hands, robes dark as night skies, the Ion mark a star upon her forehead, guiding her walk. "The King is merely a man in these halls. Only the Divine receives honor."

The girl blanches. "How should I address him, then?"

"My brother."

Onol touches a hand to her cheek as she passes. "Have peace, child. The Divine does not wish you harm."

"I understand, I will try to appear calm."

Onol forgets sometimes, the rules of the faith. They must show confidence in the Divine, never doubt or fright. The requirements of being a Priestess here, even though it is her now who oversees the priory.

"You should appear as you are, the rest will come."

The girl only bows. "High Priestess."

Onol frowns, stepping into the cool halls of the Temple.

The Ion Tree sits center of the Temple, four halls built around its massive roots. One for sleep, one for prayers and worship, one for arts and dance. The last opens into the palace gardens, available for the King alone to enter. Not that he ever visits. Onol finds her brother more often in the gardens than a place of prayer.

Sunlight is prayer to him, water and basic needs, though he will not admit it.

Raedyn claims not to pray.

Priestesses bow as she passes, Onol signs a blessing, her fingers containing the muscle memory. This is routine now.

She stops just inside the shadow of the open aired Temple hall, breath caught in her throat. It is rare she comes here; the palace view inciting panic, a clawed hand at her throat.

She can still feel it, the loss of the boughs on her head. The cutting edge of the knife held in the Sun King's hand. She remembers her screams.

Her agony.

Onol lifts her head, pushing down that little girl she used to be. There is a new King now. One of new growth. One who will never hurt her. Has never. Could never.

So why does she hesitate? Because of a title? A name that used to belong to someone she hates; faith does not allow her to hate.

Onol swallows that last bit of royal pride she carries. She steps into the light of the Flower King's gardens. Shadows slip behind her.

A path leads her straight to the palace, yet she turns to the right, slipping onto the one cutting through climbing pink roses and pale dogwood trees. Onol slows at the arch of the first tree, fingers one of the velvety blooms.

"You needn't follow me." She speaks to the shadow, who nears at her words.

"Your safety is my responsibility. Following is my duty."

"My faith is my protection."

He snorts, Onol finally allows herself to look at him. Taller than she remembers, though the boots might add to the height. Skin rich and dark as earth, eyes almond sharp and violet. Boughs twist up from his head, branching vertically into twos on

either side. One for heaven one for earth Amar
always said.

Onol tries to avoid looking at him. He's changed
so much since childhood. She doesn't want to
remember. Doesn't want to know. Doesn't want to
learn.

Yet she took the long path, the one that will take
them half a mile before they reach the palace and
she knew he would be with her every step. Perhaps
she wished for company. Perhaps *his* company- no!
Prayer in doors all day brings her melancholy, Onol
needs the sunlight, the wide blue skies, the quiet
path of roses and white trees. That is all.

"You look skinny."
A breeze takes her words, showering dogwood
petals on her hair, glimmering as stars, galaxies, in
an empty universe. Onol feels empty.

"Thank you." Amar bows. Onol snorts.

"I thought you might be happy about your
promotion, but I suppose it is terribly boring.
Guarding a Priestess who only prays all day. I
could have you transferred-"

"No. I mean- excuse me, my lady, I would like to
stay where I am. If that is also your wish."
He's fumbling. Why does her heart flip at his
voice?

Onol continues, regretting taking this path and
not wishing to look stupid turning around.

"I do not make my brother's decisions."

"Only encourage the choice of action most beneficial to you."

Onol almost stops to stare at him. "Beneficial for the Temple. Faith before kingdom."

"Country before self."

She stills before a rose trellis, arching over their heads in tiny yellow blooms and thorny vines.

"Preaching to your Priestess?" She arches a brow.

"Merely repeating a lesson."

She extends a hand from the safety of her robes, plucking a bloom from the vine.

"Ow."

"Did it cut you, my lady?"

"A prick is all. From one love to another."

"Love should not include pain."

"Yet it does. Love is pain, suffering for the sake of another."

"Love is sacrifice, yes," he takes off one of his gloves, digs in a pocket. "Love is also endurance. Passion to push through the pain and continue." Amar hands her a thin ribbon, black and soft. A gift from a lover? Why give this to her?

"For your hand, my lady. You do not want to see the King with blood on your fingers."

"Might trigger the beast." She mutters under her breath. She takes the ribbon, holding it in her fist. The cut doesn't bleed, barely got skin deep, yet every touch feels like fire to Onol. A slice through bone; her body and soul cannot handle anymore stress, now every inconvenience or discomfort is agony and fear.

A memory she still feels the wounds from.

Onol lifts the hood of her gown as she nears the palace, hiding her snubbed boughs under braided crowns and navy fabric. They all know her, the one without her crown, her mark as an Etz.

Maids bow as she passes and guards lift their chins. Their father's gilded castle is being torn apart, wealth given to the poor and hospitals and refugees from the war. Onol studies the bare walls and frameless paintings. Seems fitting, that the new King should wish a fresh start. A new look. Onol doesn't know if she agrees with Rae's fashion sense, though.

A tired man sits outside the throne room, head in his hands. He lifts his chin wearily as they near, then stands, pushing himself upright as though weighed down.

Striking, the thought that this is the man who ended their father's tyrannical reign. With a poison of stone and a broken needle.

Onol nods politely, gesturing the sign of peace. Palms extended, then the right hand circles up. *May the grounding peace of the Divine be with you. May your life be held in Divine eyes.*

Percy nods solemnly.

Amar speaks to Waiden as Onol approaches the door.

"You should get some rest, the High Priestess will counsel her brother."

"Thanks. I'm suppose to wait until he takes his next tonic, but he's refused again. He claims I will poison him, as I did…" Waiden shakes his head. "He's been in a rage since morning."

Onol sighs through her nose. She whirls on her feet. "The crown thanks you, Mr. Waiden, for your service. Get some rest."

"Princess." He bows.

The throne room doors open, Onol's sleeves trail her, draping the stone floor in navy and ultramarine. Amar five paces behind, steps crisp and uniform.

Rea paces. Boughs heavy with gold chains and dark markings painted onto his tall, regal groves and twists. He dresses in dark colors, meant to look imposing, yet only revealing his pale face and wan expression.

Her brother has not slept.

"King Raedyn." She bows, palms stretched toward him.

He stills, murmuring under his breath, then turns to her, chains swinging behind him.

His eyes widen at her guard. Odd. Raedyn is who commanded she be guarded, assigned Amar personally. Her brother's blue eyes are dark storms.

"Everyone out." He barks, collapsing on their father's throne. His throne.

The doors bang open and shut as nobles, officials and guards file from the room. Amar takes a hesitant step toward her.

"I am not to leave you." Quiet, words under his breath.

"I will be alright. Wait for me."

"Always." The words strike through her.

Raedyn waits until Amar has left, then his facade of rage falls. A weight slips from his shoulders, crashing onto the floor between them.

Onol rushes to him. No longer King of Ulna, but her brother. Her guard. Her sunshine in the storm of their life.

"What is it, brother?"

"The Stonefloor. King Silver refuses to retract it until Iliana and I are unified."

"So unify. There is no point in waiting. We are passed the mourning period, the people have accepted you, their loved Flower King."

"I have yet to restore light to Ulna. I have yet to prove myself."

"You proved yourself when you ended our father."

"I did nothing, alright." He gestures in the air. "I set a girl who had no wish to be a weapon on a powerful King and thought we would win."

"We did."

"At what cost?!" He shouts, standing, fists clenched.

"At the cost of a girl who is still alive and well." She takes a step closer. "Raedyn Vola, you saved your country, even if it was with schemes. Usis burned his own cities and was poisoning his own people." Onol shivers.

Those are being removed, too. Every work or craft built by the Sun King is being torn down. "The people must learn we cannot contain the sun without consequence. A consequence Usis was willing to have his own people pay."

"Iliana will not marry me." Rae slumps.

"What? You are betrothed."

"Were. Under pretenses. I received her help getting the poison." Rae clenches his hand. "Under the oath that she would be free afterward. I get my kingdom, she gets…opportunity."

"Opportunity?" Onol's voice flat.

"Yep." Rae sighs, looking to the ceiling. "All those ridiculous love letters were a ruse. We passed code on bringing Ulna under my rule and freeing her from Silver's grip."

"What was your plan when her mother still wanted the wedding?"

"I thought getting rid of Usis," the name a curse, "would show Radius we weren't a threat anymore. We want life, not war."

"And King Silver? She wants life?" Onol crosses her arms.

"It was Radius who proposed a match. Radius who offered peace."

"Radius who suffered under Usis's war. Radius who still poisons our ion trees with the Stonefloor though the war has been over for nearly a year. Are you sure brother, we are not still at war?"

Rae curses. "I doubt the treaty papers are even signed."

"Where is Iliana now?"

Rae's eyes drift skyward, he opens his mouth, then snarls. ***"You have too much power over me, sister."***

"I mean only to help you, Raedyn. You asked for my council." Onol takes a step back, Rae's voice holding a new tone, one voice over laying the other.

"You command me to war again?!" Her brother's fists curl, hands like jagged claws.

"I ask you to see truth, to find sense." Her voice sharp. She lowers it. "I ask you examine every possibility before reaching a conclusion. Please, Rea, you frighten me."

His eyes widen, the King staggers back as if struck.

He looks away from her, stammering, gasping. "I-I'm sorry-y, s-sister." His hands tremble and he collapses before the throne.

"Raedyn!" Onol lifts his arms, struggling with his weight.

"I'm fine." He waves a dismissing hand, ringed and heavy.

"You're not. You need rest. You need to listen to Waiden. You need-"

"Don't tell me what to do!" His eyes go bloodshot. Near red. Onol drops his arms, backing away.

"Guards!" Onol tries to keep the shriek from her voice yet it slips through.

Amar is the first to enter, followed by the King's.

"The King is unwell. He needs rest. Please, see him abed and the physician brought." She swallows hard, Rae's red eyes still locked on hers.

"Yes, High Priestess." The guards bow their heads, helping Rae to his feet though he barks at them to release him. Amar stops at her side, his heat reaching through her fear, soothing.

"Are you well?"

"Simply worried. I shall return to prayer."

They leave the throne room with a flurry of sleeves and Amar's hand close yet not touching her back. Onol cannot help her next thoughts, though they seep chill into her bones.

Something is wrong with the King.

www.ingramcontent.com/pod-product-compliance
Lightning Source LLC
Chambersburg PA
CBHW031003260626
47169CB00002B/669